He looked down and shivered

Five hundred feet below, the construction workers looked like ants, the forklift trucks like scale models.

He began to feel dizzy; he hated heights. He should never have agreed to meet anyone up here. He was thinking about returning to ground level when he heard a noise behind him. He started to turn— and felt a blow that knocked him off balance.

He staggered on the edge of the platform, desperately trying to grab something to pull him to safety. But someone pushed him again, and he fell.

Hugh Zachary
is also the author
of Raven House Mystery
To Guard the Right

A robbery gone bad—
that's what it looked like.

The retired admiral had been tied and
tortured, but he wouldn't talk. So
they left him to drown in a bathtub.

The local police had no leads. Soon
the case would be thrown into
"Pending" and forgotten.

Then a very exclusive organization
took an interest—a society of
vigilantes who carried on when the
police gave up. Their methods were
unorthodox but successful. Whoever
had killed the old man would suffer
for it. And suffer grievously.

Hugh Zachary

TOP LEVEL DEATH

A RAVEN HOUSE MYSTERY FROM

W RLDWIDE

TORONTO · NEW YORK · LOS ANGELES · LONDON

Raven House edition published August 1982.

Second printing

ISBN 0-373-63044-1

Printed in Canada

1

IT WAS A LONG CLIMB from ground level. The core jacket in the nuclear reactor was a cylinder that extended upward for five hundred feet, anchored in place by its one-hundred-foot base extending into the sublevels below ground. And the man hated heights.

He didn't like riding the crowded elevator, either, so he climbed flights of stairs, detoured through the usual chaos where men and equipment moved in seemingly random motion through and around mazes of huge and small pipes. A small group of pipe fitters worked behind draped sheets of plastic, torches hissing, the hiss only a part of the noise that constantly bombarded the ears in a steady droning, clanking, hissing roar. It took a new man a week or so just to find his way around. She was one helluva big mother, was the Tristate reactor, and she'd been under construction for six years with no end in sight.

It wasn't difficult to understand why things moved slowly. People stood with coffee cups in hand discussing baseball scores. On level five a crane operator lowered a boiler and banged it hard, so that the clang made him wince. He made a mental note to check the piece carefully. That particular piece of hardware wasn't in his section, but, by God, his kids might be going to school in Petertown before he moved on, and he didn't want to see this mother going on the line with a strained seam in a boiler. When steam is under the normal pressures in a B.W.R.—a boiling-water reactor—all you need is a pinhole-sized weakness and you've got problems.

He stayed away from the open equipment bays. Just to think of looking down made his stomach queasy. Once he had to walk out and around some equipment being moved, and he couldn't keep his eyes away, looked down, down, down, all the way to the concrete floor that was littered with machinery, crawling with men who already looked very small, and he wasn't even at the top.

Fortunately, his area of responsibility was on the first couple of levels and outside the containment building. He didn't often go to the top. He didn't like the reason he was making his way slowly upward, but told himself it wasn't all bad, climbing the stairwells. He was in his thirties and he had a spare tire hanging over his leather belt with the Indian silver-and-turquoise buckle, so the exercise would be good for him.

He was breathing hard when he gave up at a

level one hundred feet below the top and waited for the elevator. He nodded to some workmen as the door opened. One man spoke to him by name.

The dome at the top of the reactor vessel was shrouded in plastic, and behind the shielding semitransparent curtain he could see and hear the torches working. He walked near the curved outer wall of the containment shell. Aside from the pipe fitters behind the plastic curtain he saw no one. He halted. There was an expression of impatience on his face as he lighted a cigarette.

The open bay seemed to draw him with a malevolent force, causing his heart to pump. The evil force took him three, four steps forward until he could look down. He knew that he shouldn't, but he was unable to resist, just as a man who is afraid of snakes cannot walk away as he stands mesmerized in front of a reptile pit.

Five hundred feet down the hard-hatted men were toy-sized. A forklift that looked like a skillfully constructed model moved across the floor. Sounds of construction were funneled upward through the open bays to clang and roar in his ears. Then, sharply, everything seemed to shift position. He was falling.

Nature was kind, as she is when a small animal is seized by fang or claw, shock moving in swiftly to deaden pain and terror, allowing only the one quick scream of terminal agony.

A worker was disobeying safety rules and was taking a shortcut across the floor directly under the open equipment bays. He felt the shock wave, a brief jolt not unlike that blast of air one feels when being passed in a small car by a fully laden semi, and then the dreadful sound of impact. The worker's clothing was spattered by exploding blood.

2

DRIVING A VOLKSWAGEN CAMPER VAN northward out of the gorge demanded a bull market of shifting up and down. The grades weren't severe, but the van was a bit underpowered. The hills were desolately impressive under the August sun, barren, brown, drab, but he was in the mood for such desolate places. He had promised himself a month of it, and he was sorry that he'd decided on the camper instead of a four-wheeler. Interesting little dirt roads branched off and climbed hills or fell into barren valleys, inviting but inaccessible to the cumbersome van. He was in no particular hurry. He had sent word to those who might or might not be concerned to forget him for at least thirty days and perhaps more. He had some thinking to do. It had become a bit sticky in Phoenix, and for the first time he'd hesitated, not knowing doubt, but somewhat alienated, sick of it, sated with death and blood and violence.

It was that hesitation that caused the doubt to grow in his mind; not doubt about the justice of punishing a man who had kidnapped, raped, mutilated a woman who, because she was ambitious, energetic, self-confident, held a job that required her to do a lot of traveling alone. No, the doubt did not extend to his basic belief that one who took life in the most brutal of fashions deserved the same treatment. It was doubt in himself, for the moment had come, and he'd hesitated, and the murderer had run. Time and money had been spent in tracking down a killer who would never have been caught by police agencies, and he'd received the assignment and set up the end of it carefully, knowing that he'd have only one chance. And then he'd questioned his right to kill, for only a moment, and the opportunity had passed and he allowed himself to be seen with the killer, to be associated with the man in the eyes of several competent witnesses. He had not even been able to follow when the killer bolted, had been forced to call for help.

He didn't like thinking about it, the way he'd failed, but it was something he had to do. Next time he hesitated, the outcome might be less satisfactory. Next time there might not be another operative nearby to finish the job. Next time he might hesitate and feel the stunning power of a bullet in his gut.

The air conditioner in the van had a tendency to freeze his legs and leave his upper body to broil in the sun. It was above ninety outside, the sun blazing down from a sky devoid of cloud to reflect off the bleak countryside. He saw a road

sign that showed a low mileage to Petertown and
he still was not sure he'd stop there. He was
bound for a destination north of the Petertown
area, up past Windfall Lake.

He had dawdled through the gorge looking at
waterfalls and high cliffs that showed, hundreds
of feet up, the marks of a prehistoric flood, and
had spent the previous night in a beauty of a
campsite. There'd been a fine view of the river,
and the evening had settled into a coolness that
should have made sleep a pleasure. He had not
discovered until he was all set up, a steak beginning to make smoke on the grill, why the park was
nearly empty. What had to be the busiest railroad
in the world ran past the camp just below, between his riverside parking space and the water.
He estimated at least one train per hour throughout the night, and each one sounded as if it were
going to blast its way directly through his
camper.

At least if he stopped in Petertown he could
find a real bed, and he'd be damned sure that
there wasn't a railroad within five miles.

He entered the town from the south, avoiding
the interstate. He wandered around a bit before
he found a motel and asked for a room away from
traffic noise. He mixed bourbon and ginger ale,
punched two pillows into shape behind his head
and sipped as he studied the map. He wanted to
see the falls up north. There the prehistoric river,
fed by a glacial torrent, poured over cliffs three

times higher than Niagara and miles wide. It would be an easy day's drive, so what the hell. But old Frank would be mad if he ever found out his old buddy had been right there in Petertown and had not called. He picked up the telephone book.

The voice that answered the telephone was soft, all girl. He had met her once, briefly, when he had flown into North Florida during a heat wave to stand in a church with no air conditioning and hear Frank Pitt say, "I do," and then to kiss a tall slim girl with a crisp accent he had not been able to place.

"Belinda?" he asked. "Belinda Pitt?"

"Who's calling, please?" He had heard TV pitchwomen speak that way, overemphasizing each sound, making it come out as more than all-American.

"G.W. Smith," he said. "I know it's inconsiderate to call without advance notice, but I happen to be nearby and I haven't seen Frank—and you—since the wedding."

There was a long pause. "You're Tusk, right?"

"Right."

"I remember. Tall, sandy haired—"

"And ugly," he said with a chuckle.

"Frank talked about you so much." He didn't, at first, catch the past tense. "You're nearby?"

"The Holiday Inn."

She gave him brisk no-nonsense instructions. He asked her to wait while he got pen and paper.

"If you can make it by six," she said, "I'll add on a steak for you."

The house was on the northern slope of a barren hill. A lush lawn contrasted with the brownness of the surroundings. New houses were going up all around. An I.H. Scout sat high on big all-weather tires in the driveway. The garage doors were open, showing quantities of cardboard boxes. It looked as if Frank were going Gypsy again. It was the nature of his business. He was one of the good ones in a fraternity of unusual men; men who, in a huge and technical field, formed a cadre of experts always in demand, getting job offers in Venezuela, Saudi Arabia, Mexico, odd corners of the United States, wherever the billions of dollars could be accumulated to start construction of a nuclear generating plant.

Tusk walked by slinging his feet forward, as if the feet carried themselves by their own weight. The lawn had been freshly cut. Sprinklers were working and there was a moist grassy smell mixed with a hint of charcoal smoke. She came around the side of the house. She was dressed in shorts and halter, slim and tall as he remembered her, flaxen hair pulled back into a ponytail.

"I'm in back," she said. "Come on around."

He dodged a sprinkler and entered the backyard through a gate in a redwood-stained basketweave fence. There was a small swimming pool and a patio and another area of surprisingly lush grass.

"I'm a vodka freak," she said. She had not smiled. "I also have Scotch."

"Whatever you're having."

A rolling table served as a bar. He looked at the grill to see that the charcoal was about ready, took the glass. "Cheers," she said.

"You're looking great, Belinda."

Now there was a small smile. "No one has called me Belinda for years."

"Oh?"

"Lindy, mostly. Frank sometimes called me Beast."

He grinned. Back in another age, when the world was a nicer and less complicated place, Frank would say, "The beasts are on the loose. Let's go and snatch a couple." Meaning girls. And Frank didn't feel that way at all. He loved them, all the little darlings, fell in love at least once a week, went steady with two girls at a time until he got caught. Well, he'd had the equipment to get away with it, a tall, handsome, slim kid with a rifle arm. Even in high school he could fire a football almost the length of the field.

But Tusk's mind was not in complete hibernation. "That's twice you've used the past tense in speaking of Frank," he said. He wasn't concerned. He'd seen the signs of moving in the garage. Perhaps Frank had gone ahead to another job. Perhaps he'd just gone. Things like that happened, even to tall pretty girls with flaxen hair and nice eyes.

She'd been standing quite near and now she turned, walked away, removed the aluminum foil that covered two steaks.

Something came to mar the smell of newly mowed grass, the warm sun. "What is it, Lindy?" he asked.

Her voice was just audible. "Frank's dead."

Words can have so many shades of meaning. Tusk Smith had many reasons for death words to have special meaning. And it was not the first time he had known that jar, that sinking inside, when the word "dead" is applied suddenly to a friend.

"I deliberately did not tell you on the phone," she said. "I wanted to tell you in person, because you were something special to him. You know that, don't you?"

"We grew up together." What could he say?

Neither he nor Frank had been much for writing letters. The last he'd heard was a telephone call to tell him of another gypsying, of the move to Petertown, the address and telephone number. How long? A year? You go through life having only a damned small number of friends and they seem to be always going their own ways, but you know that they're there and you can pick up the telephone and say meaningless things. "Hey, what's happening?" But you know they're there, and then you hear one word that means they are not there, not anymore.

"When?" he asked.

"Two weeks." She moved gracefully, plopped steak onto hot metal. There was smoke and a quick sizzling sound.

"Jesus, Lindy."

"It's all right. I can talk about it now. He fell."

Well, maybe she was ready to talk, but there was another silence and he didn't break it, because he was thinking of Frank and in his own way saying goodbye, thinking of something Frank had said a long time ago. It was after a very rough football game, and they had dressed and were walking across the empty grid. Frank pointed upward to the stands. He was walking with difficulty, because a big defensive tackle had tried to tear his leg off.

"The only reason why I come out here to get my head broken," Frank had said, "is so I won't have to sit up there." He couldn't even stand to climb the stands, with all that solidity of rock under him.

"I can't imagine Frank getting high enough off the ground to fall."

"I know," she said. She turned to face him. "But there were times when he had to. He was good at his job." Her eyes were large, glistening. "He fell five hundred feet."

He moved to her, put a hand on her shoulder. Her bare skin seemed to be chilled. "All right," he said. "Maybe you aren't ready to talk, after all."

"I have to sooner or later."

"Not on an empty stomach," he said. He took up the tools. "I just happen to be the foremost expert in the Western world on charcoaled steaks. You mix, I'll be chef."

It is good policy, even when it seems to be thoughtlessness, to get the survivors to talk about themselves, to sidetrack, for even a few moments, the quick and sudden alteration of a world, to shove death into a corner and know it's there but ignore it.

"It's a nice house," he said. "A beautiful lawn."

"The earth is rich," she said. "It grows anything. All you have to do is pour water on it. We're on the irrigation line."

"Funny, I never think of this area as having high desert."

"I know. You think of snow-covered mountains and cool rain forests."

She had finished mixing a second round. "I like it here," she said.

"Going to stay?"

"For the time being, at least. I have my job. Frank wasn't one hundred percent in favor of my working, but he didn't really mind. And God knows we found uses for the money. You can't imagine how expensive it is here. They think the land is pure gold, and building costs are unbelievable."

"I know how much they charge for a motel room," he said.

"You should have called here first. There's plenty of room." She flushed and looked away.

"You don't have to tell me that's not an invitation," he said.

"Thanks," she responded with that tiny smile. "I guess it's a sort of battle fatigue. Men don't lose much time, you know. 'Look, Lindy, if there's anything I can do, like warm your empty bed.'"

He grinned. "Nice fellows all, though. Real friends."

"I guess I feel that I *really* know you, Tusk," she said.

"If there's anything *I* can do.... I saw some packing operations in the garage. If you need a strong back—"

"Thanks. It's mostly finished. It's mostly some things Frank wanted sent to his family."

That didn't sound like Frank. Frank had been one of those who planned to live forever. "He thought that far ahead?" he asked.

She nodded, looked upward toward the crest of the hill where the falling sun was going molten gold. "He began to change. Job pressure, maybe. This job was a jump ahead for him, a big jump. He had two graduate engineers working under him. The plant is a disaster area, years behind schedule, and you know Frank. He had to take on responsibility for everything. He took it upon himself to fight everyone, root out sloppy work, to think of the money being wasted as his own.

He was taking night classes, too. He was about ready to be licensed. And the Feds were making things difficult. They were trying to make rulings that said a man without a degree couldn't do certain jobs, even if he had the experience and the ability, like Frank. That was worrying him, and that was one of the main reasons why he was studying for his professional license. With the license he would be the equal of a man with any number of degrees."

He spoke into the silence that followed. "He changed, you said."

"Oh, just overwork, I guess. He was always so uptight."

"How did it happen, Lindy?" he asked. She had sat down in a lawn chair. He stood over the sizzling steaks.

"No one really knows. He was alone. He'd probably gone up to inspect the welds on the outer shell of the reactor vessel. A man was supposed to meet him up there, but he was delayed."

"And he just fell?"

She shrugged.

"But he had come to believe that he was, after all, mortal?" he asked.

"Something like that," she said. "He increased his insurance just a few months ago. And he went to a lawyer. He had a will, and the first I knew of it was when he gave me a copy to put into the safety-deposit box."

"Nosy question, Lindy. Are you all right for money?"

"The insurance seems like a lot, but you know what's happening with the dollar. I guess I don't really have to work just now. Every time I drive out there and see the building I ask myself why. I have to look at it. It's there, that damned reactor—"

"You work out at the plant, then?"

"I, sir, am a lady cop. At least, a sort of cop. I'm a security guard."

"I'll bet you look good in uniform," he said, to lighten it a bit, for her eyes were misting again.

The steaks were delicious, the wine cold, the evening tapering down from the heat of the day to become pleasant. A light breeze came down from the hill. He found himself carrying the conversational load, talking more than usual, telling her about the time in Saigon when he saw Frank walking down the street in uniform. He quickly gathered up a dozen business ladies, gave them a few bucks each, and stood laughing his head off when all twelve of them descended on Frank and started clinging, kissing, feeling. He talked about the time he and Frank had the fight over a cute little cheerleader, about Frank's agonized refusal to go into the army with him, choosing the navy instead, for it was Tusk's avowed goal to go airborne. Frank had never set foot in an airplane and didn't intend to.

It took him a long time to make her laugh, as

the darkness gathered and hid the barren hills, while the sprinklers added moisture to the air. Her laugh was a ripple of sound that filled the fenced yard.

Later she asked, "Want to stay here?"

"And scandalize the neighbors?"

"I don't care. I don't even know them."

"I guess not, Lindy."

"I'm home about five-thirty," she said, "if the traffic is no worse than usual. I cook a mean chicken dish with lots of spices and lemon and ripe olives. You dip your bread into the juices."

"Later," he said. "I think I should fly down to San Diego."

She nodded. "Yes, well. I have talked to her, of course, and I've written to her."

"How'd she take it?" he asked.

"No tears. At least not on the telephone." She sighed. "Please come back. I won't weep, I promise. It's just that you're the first person I've been able to talk with."

"I'll call when I get back from San Diego. That will give you notice to begin that chicken thing you cook." He'd have to come back to Petertown to get the van.

She led him through the house. The sudden light caused both of them to squint. At the door she stood on tiptoe to kiss him on the cheek. She seemed pale and her touch was so cool. She was, he began to realize, a very beautiful woman.

"You're good company, sir," she said. "I

know now why Frank was always talking about you."

"Most of it was lies," he replied.

He caught an Air West commuter plane, changed at Sea-Tac, landed in Southern California heat, taxied to a beach area to find a mobile home with a shaded portico in front and a patio in back. She was not at home. There was a note on the door: "Gone diving. Back soon." He sat down in a comfortable rocker and put his feet up on the wooden side of a planter. Petunias bloomed wildly there, the sun was warm, and he dozed.

"G.W. Smith." The voice came to him from out of the past, strong, chiding. "Get your big feet out of my petunias!"

For a moment, as he awakened, he was seventeen again. He dropped his feet with a clunk, saying, "Yes, ma'am."

She was carrying a twin-tank scuba rig and looked far too frail, her body all bones and protrusions in her wet suit, her knees knobby, old thighs stringy. Her gray hair was cropped short and was still damp. But her eyes were so alive, twinkling.

"It's about time you came to see me," she said, putting down the tanks, clasping him wetly, smelling of salt water.

"I just found out," he said. "As a matter of fact, I didn't know until I went through Petertown to visit him."

"God damn it, G.W.," she said. "It's bad enough when you outlive your children. It's incredibly unfair when you outlast your only grandson.''

"Well," he said, "I wanted to see you, Mandy, as much for myself as for you, I have to admit.''

"Feel sort of alone, huh?" she asked. He nodded. "Well, come on in. Let me get out of this modern girdle.''

The living room was surprisingly large. It overlooked the sea. "There's booze in the kitchen, if you've become a daylight drinker.''

"No, thanks.''

"Well, just cool it while I get dressed.''

It took her only a few minutes, another minute or two to mix instant tea and deliver it in a tall glass. She sat down opposite him. "You saw Lindy, I guess.''

He nodded.

"And?''

"She's adjusting," he said.

"Humph," she snorted.

He didn't question that "humph." She'd say what she had to say when she wanted to say it. Mandy Pitt was that sort of woman. There'd been a time when he felt more at home in the Pitt house than in his own, and she had been, at least in the eyes of a teenage boy, ancient even then. Good Lord, how old was she? Seventy? Eighty? Carrying two scuba tanks.

"What did Miss Lindy tell you?" Mandy asked.

"That he fell five hundred feet from the top of the containment building.''

"Did she tell you that he was expecting something to happen?"

"She said he'd been tense, moody, had made out a will."

"Does that sound like Frank to you?" Mandy asked.

"Mandy, it does not sound like Frank," he said.

"More tea?" He shook his head, no. "Just sit tight for a minute, then." She was up and away, moving briskly, and came back with a letter.

"You've changed your life-style," he observed, looking around the antiseptic, modern, impersonal room. The Pitt house had been almost like a museum, full of antique wood and lace, oak sideboards and walnut beds, tintypes and Persian rugs.

"Didn't know what it meant to be free," she said, "until I got rid of all that junk that owned me." She sat, extended the letter. "Just the last part. The rest is the usual Pitt jive, smart-ass kid trying to make an old woman's last days happy."

He knew the scrawled, masculine handwriting, could almost hear Frank's voice. Once he'd let that smooth-talking bastard talk him into making a tour of duty down a river. Frank had asked for the river duty, coming in from a safe-missile destroyer out in the gulf to help clear the Cong out of the delta. Tusk up to that point had thought that the jungle was bad. Down there in the delta it was more difficult to distinguish the Cong from the friendlies, and every bend in the river brought with it the possibility of ambush, of a sudden and deadly outbreak of automatic-weapons fire. Frank loved it, laughed at Tusk's nervousness.

But now he was reading words written by a man whose blood had exploded out of his crushed body to soil a few square yards of cement.

> Mandy, I always thought, when I thought about it at all, that I'd outlast you, but now I'm not so sure. Maybe we'll both be lucky and live another hundred years, but just between me and you, and I wouldn't say this to anyone else, I've had this eerie and strange feeling of late. I don't want to be maudlin, but if anything happens to me I want you to buy yourself a fifth of the best and have one last one for me, and don't bother to stir your rusty old bones to come up here for the funeral. Just remember me and talk to—

A word had been scratched out, but not completely. The word was "Tusk." Frank had re-written it in Mandy's language, "G.W."

Mandy had risen and was reading over his shoulder. "Why would he want me to talk to you?" she asked.

He didn't answer immediately. He himself was having an eerie and strange feeling. Finally he said, "I guess he knew it would hit me hard, Mandy."

"He had a will made out. Left me ten thousand bucks' worth of insurance." She sat down again, the old faded eyes seeming to study his face. "Why would a man in his prime make out an insurance policy to a seventy-five-year-old woman?"

"Mandy, we both know he didn't commit suicide," he said.

"Bet your sweet ass he didn't," she said. "He *knew* something was wrong, G.W. He could feel it. He wanted you to do something about it. You were a military cop for a while, weren't you?"

"Before the general came over and wanted me to play soldier with him," Tusk said.

"He knew something," she insisted. "And he wanted you to do something."

"It was investigated," he said. "They called it an accident."

"G.W., you know and I know that if Frank ever had to put himself five hundred feet up in the air he'd be hanging onto something with all hands and his tail. Frank and I were talking about you, just this past spring when I was up there, and he said he thought you were doing some kind of investigative work. Is that right?"

"Wrong," he said quickly. He couldn't remember ever saying anything to Frank that would have made him even suspect what line of work he was in. "Dead wrong. I am retired. I'm on medical disability. I have an interest in a housing development in North Carolina with a couple of nice kids, and they're making me more money than I thought was in the world.''

She sighed. ''All right, G.W. Play it close if you want to. He asked me to talk to you and I have. Whatever happens now, it won't bring him back. I'm too damned old to think in terms of revenge. Maybe it was an accident. Maybe he was just overworking. But if you should decide to do something—''

''I'm going back up there, see Lindy again, pick up my van and get lost,'' he said.

''Well, if you should decide to stick around up there for a little while you'll need a place to stay and someone to talk with, someone who knows the territory.'' She reached for pen and paper. ''I met this old gal last spring. She's a crazy old broad who goes off climbing up mountains, but she's got some sense left and she rents clean rooms.''

''Climbing mountains any worse than swimming with sharks at the age of seventy-five?'' he asked, deadpan.

''Don't be a smart-ass,'' she said.

3

A BEAUTIFUL WOMAN in a brown skirt and white halter top sat easily before a walnut table so cleverly jointed that one could not find the seams. Her skin was darkened by sun. A slit in the skirt revealed a strong and shapely leg. Her hands were folded in her lap. For the assignment just finished she had allowed her hair to return to its natural tawny, sun-streaked state.

She looked directly into the mirror in front of her. Her voice was low as she added her oral report to the written report, which had been duplicated so that a copy lay in front of each of the four men who sat in individual cubicles behind the one-way mirror. The judge, in his seventies, wore a neat off-white suit. He listened to the calm voice with a mixture of emotions. It had been a cruel and difficult case, and it had taken more than two years to bring it to conclusion.

When the woman finished, the coordinator, always the spokesman, said, "Thank you, Zed. Are there any further questions, gentlemen?"

"None," said the prosecutor.

"No," the judge said.

The fourth man did not speak.

"I have one further comment," said the woman known as Zed. "For the second time in two years an operation went badly, gentlemen. For the second time in two years I have been called upon to come to the aid of an operative. Oddly enough, it was the same operative in both cases."

"You are speaking of Tee," answered the prosecutor.

"Tee," she said. "One such incident is understandable. But two in two years?"

The fourth man never spoke in a normal voice. The coordinator, youngest of the four, had long been certain of the identity of the prosecutor. The prosecutor's voice was a giveaway, for it was often heard on the media. The coordinator was about half-sure of the identity of the judge. About the fourth man he was, and had always been, totally in the dark.

The fourth man's voice was whispery, deliberately disguised. "Your observations have been noted. And since you have spoken of it, there is another matter that touches on the subject. Mr. Coordinator?"

A slit opened on Zed's side of the mirror and ejected a sheet of paper. She picked it up and held it close to her eyes. Reading glasses were for use in privacy. She took her time, and as she read the coordinator felt, once again, the urge to leap up and break through the partition; to know, at last, the identity of the fourth man.

Zed had finished. "He is much too personally involved. Moreover, there is no hard evidence that a crime has been committed."

"I must agree," said the coordinator.

"Your positions are noted," the fourth man whispered. "However, I would like to remind all of you, and especially you, Zed, that Tee has been and is the best we have. There is no chauvinism involved, Zed, for you are the second best. I find no faults in Tee's judgment in either of the two assignments during which he had to ask for help. In fact, there is not one of you who has not at one time or another called for assistance."

"Your reminder is noted," Zed answered coldly.

"If the request we make of you is too much of an imposition," the whispery voice went on, "or if you feel you cannot work well with Tee, I expect you to so state."

Zed sighed, mentally saying goodbye to a month in the Jamaican sun. "It is not an imposition," she said. "I can work with Tee."

"Good," the fourth man said.

"Actually," the coordinator said, "we are asking you merely to remain alert and available. As you pointed out, there is no proof that a crime has been committed. If Tee's work should indicate a need for action, it would not be advisable for him to activate a solution, because of his personal involvement.''

''I can be alert on the North Shore,'' Zed said.

''That is agreeable,'' the coordinator said. ''Please check with Oscar during each forty-eight-hour period.''

''Yes,'' she said.

''Thank you,'' the fourth man whispered. She knew they were finished with her. She heard a relay click, knew that there would be no further sound from the speakers and that if she spoke she would not be heard. She left the cubicle. Oscar met her outside. He was dressed impeccably, as usual.

''I will be in the usual place,'' she told him. ''I will call you tomorrow and each second morning thereafter.''

''Very good,'' Oscar said.

She gave him a cold smile. ''We need a code word.''

Oscar was the only face she had ever seen in the facility. She would leave the building via a windowless boarding tunnel, fly in a jet with permanently blacked windows.

''I have put some thought into it,'' he said.

''Judging from the twinkle in your eye it must be a clever one.''

''L search for some little significance in these matters,'' Oscar said. ''Would Manhattan be suitable to you?''

"Inspired, Oscar," she smiled. "Definitely inspired."

In his cubicle the coordinator summed up the concluded case, gave an accounting of funds expended, noted that final payment had been made.

"Speaking of payment," the prosecutor asked, "who is the client in Washington?"

"There is one unusual aspect there," the whispery voice said. "I have indicated that I wish to go along with the wishes of a very good operative, but I would listen to your opinion, since in this case the client and the operative are one and the same."

The prosecutor laughed. He knew that the services of the organization did not come cheaply. "Maybe we should have invested in that housing development in North Carolina after all," he said.

"I don't begrudge Tee's business sense," the fourth man said. "The question is, should we put the facilities of the organization at his disposal?"

"I say yes, without hesitation," the judge said.

"Yes," agreed the prosecutor.

"Unanimous," the coordinator said.

"We conclude one task and another springs up," the fourth man said in his whispered voice. "It never ends. We have concluded another, gentlemen, and, as is our custom, I will now ask you to join me in a moment of silent meditation."

The coordinator bowed his head. After a few

moments of silence the hoarse voice spoke. "It has ended, and it begins. May we continue, in the words of Abraham Lincoln, to live with malice toward none; with charity for all; with firmness in the right, as God gives us to see the right. Let us strive on to finish the work we are in; to bind up the nation's wounds; to care for him who shall have borne the battle, and for his widow, and his orphan—to do all that may achieve and cherish a just and lasting peace among ourselves."

The coordinator sighed. He would be the last to leave. The others would go on ahead, faces never seen. He thought about the words from Lincoln and chuckled grimly. With malice toward none? None save the guilty and the unpunished.

Far out in the Arizona desert—with luck, never to be found—was the deteriorating body of a man who had kidnapped and mutilated the body of a female employee of the Texas Citrus Commission just over two years ago; a man who had gone unpunished, a man who would never have been apprehended by law officials. He had been discovered through a routine police report of a casual arrest, through his fingerprints, and traced to his cheap lodgings in Phoenix. He had there been judged, questioned and found guilty.

"An eye for an eye," the coordinator said, knowing that he would not be heard.

The fourth man had left off the usual prayer. Did the fourth man, too, feel a bit weak as he looked into the beautiful face of that dark

woman with the tawny and sun-streaked hair,
perhaps picturing her at the moment of final
decision, after the murderer had escaped the tall
man who had found him? Did the fourth man feel
that calling upon God in the presence of that
woman was, perhaps, a bit cynical?

4

ANNA LARCH was a tall spare woman dressed in Levi's, a plaid shirt and hiking boots. Her frame was trim with not an ounce of excess fat, and her skin had the dry sun-browned look of a habitual and heedless outdoorswoman. She examined the big sandy-haired man who stood on the stoop of her aging frame house, his alert brown eyes squinted against the brightness of the August sun.

"Well, you're a big one," she said. He was. He stood well over six feet. He had the bulk, she thought, of a good linebacker, reappraised him quickly, decided that he was more the modern, swift, big tight-end type.

"My name is Smith," he said. "I have been told that you have a room for rent."

"Ladies only," she replied.

"Mandy Pitt told me you sometimes make an exception to that rule."

"What are you to that old bird?"

"Aside from being in love with her all my life," Tusk said, smiling, noting the laugh lines around the woman's mouth and eyes, "she practically raised me."

"Come in," Anna said.

The living room was small, and made to seem smaller by an incredible array of items ranging from a dollhouse under construction to a sofa half-covered with books, a piece of driftwood, Indian artifacts and loose papers. She shoved things out of the way, motioned him to a seat on the uncovered portion of the sofa, sat down in the one leather-bound chair and pulled a cigarette from the pocket of her shirt.

"Smoke?" she asked.

He shook his head. He saw only one ashtray, nailed to the arm of her chair. "Only way I can keep up with the damned thing," she said, waving a hand at the chaos of the room. "So Mandy Pitt sent you. That would make you a friend of Frank Pitt's."

"It would," Tusk said.

"How long would you want the room?"

"It's hard to say," he said.

She grinned, blew smoke from her nose in a curiously old-fashioned way. "One of those," she said. "Construction bum."

"I guess you could say that," he said.

"Got a job?"

"Not just yet."

"Shouldn't be a problem."

He'd made a couple of telephone calls about that, as a matter of fact, and somewhere in the state a union card was being made up with his name on it.

"I can pay two weeks in advance," he said.

"Don't worry about it. I guess it won't ruin my reputation any more than it's been ruined. But don't you want to see the room?"

"Sure."

In contrast to the living room, the room off the rear, with an outside entry on the back porch, was neat, contained a bed, a chair, a chest of drawers, a small lady's desk, a lamp and a spindle-backed desk chair.

"No kitchen privileges," she said.

"I'm not much of a cook."

"Neither am I." She had an open laugh, throaty, head thrown back to reveal the stringy tendons of her neck. "Bath is private. You want female visitors, just be sure they're quiet."

"I don't anticipate any," he said with a grin.

"Don't see why not," she said. "If I were ten years younger—"

"Now watch it," he said. "I have this fatal weakness for older women."

"Mandy still fooling around underwater?" she asked, changing the subject as she led him back out onto the porch.

"She's quite a gal," he said.

"I do make a respectable pot of coffee," she said, "if you like it strong. Come in and tell me about her."

As they talked she worked on a dress, sitting

with a straight back on a stool in front of an ancient sewing machine. It was not difficult, he
found, after bringing her up to date on Mandy, to
get her talking about herself. She was, she open-
ly admitted, fifty-seven. She'd given up serious
mountain climbing only two years before, after,
she said, "falling all the way down the damned
mountain."

"Still like to get out," she said. "Not like it
used to be. I'd take my girls—" she'd been a
scout leader, had never had children of her own
"—and just start out. Can't do that now. Fences,
irrigation ditches. Half the damned state turned
into national parks and full of dingbats from the
cities. Can't even gather wood for a campfire."

"It looks as if prosperity has come to the area,"
Tusk replied.

"If you can call it that," she said. "I just say
too many people. Started back in the war when
the Feds began to build out at Sweetwater. First
just a little old reactor to make bombs, then
more. Got half the desert closed off now. I don't
know how many thousand people on the roads.
Don't try driving mornings or evenings when
they're coming and going from work. Secret
government stuff up on Jericho Mountain. Used
to have the best view around here, and now you
can't even go up there."

"Are you a native?" he asked.

"No. I came here a hundred or so years ago.
Just after Lewis and Clark looked down on this

valley and said that it would never be capable of supporting civilized life. Then they started pumping water.'' She shrugged. ''I'm still not sure there's civilized life around here. Whores walking the streets in Midland and the police so busy they don't even bother with them. Every nuclear company in the United States has built out at Sweetwater. People come from all over the world. The jails are full. The city of Midland is suing a judge because he turned a drunk loose after his second drunk-driving conviction. State law says that's a mandatory ninety days in the jug, but the judge said there wasn't room in jail for him.''

Tusk nodded. He'd seen impacted areas before, boom towns. The first thing that happened was overloading and overwork for the law-enforcement agencies. No one would have had the time or the interest to investigate what seemed to be a routine fatal accident on a big construction site outside of town.

''The telephone company can't handle the demand,'' Anna went on. ''And the banks will tell you that their computers are hopelessly behind. Lots of places won't take checks, because even if the check is good the overworked computers might bounce it and at best not get it cleared for weeks. Living costs are at least a third higher than in other parts of the country.''

''Lots of work, though,'' Tusk said.

''Which brings up something. You don't talk

and you don't look like your typical construction bum." Her alert brown eyes were squinting at him. "Frank Pitt's pretty little widow have anything to do with your being here?"

He grinned. "We're good friends," he said. Might as well let her think that Lindy was his reason for staying.

"You're not married," she stated. "I can tell."

"No."

"Well, just remember this," she said. "A woman loses her man and the first thing that happens is all the good old friends think they'll do her a favor, make her forget."

"Do I look the type?" he asked.

"No. Can't say you do. But I've been there. Men we'd known for years, when my John died...." She looked out the window, looked back, gave him that throaty laugh. "Then, when you might like to have one of them around—"

He rose. "Anna, I'm going to leave before you start giving me ideas."

She laughed again. "Sure, sure. Must be some Irish in you. You've got the smile, the blarney."

He paid her for two weeks in advance, moved some basic necessities in from the camper. The bathtub was spotlessly clean and he soaked for a long time, letting the warm water soothe the always tender stumps of his legs, heavy artificial feet sitting beside the bed. When he got out of the tub he knee-walked over, strapped on his feet and dressed.

He looked for a telephone booth as he drove away from Anna Larch's house, did not see one, decided that he'd just drop in on Lindy. There was a big chunk of Detroit iron in her driveway, a New Yorker, new and splendid. He hesitated before parking the camper on the street, then decided that it would be the natural thing for him to stop by and tell the widow of his old friend, that he was going to stay on for a while and, work a bit to replenish his traveling funds.

She was in shorts and halter, her long shapely legs showing an even tan. Her face was blank at first, and then she smiled. "You're back," she said. "Please come in."

The man seated on the couch in the living room was wearing about four hundred dollars' worth of lightweight suit, had a fashionable haircut and a round face behind black horn-rim glasses. The look he gave Tusk was hardly a welcome.

"This is Mr. Martin," Lindy said. "Mr. Martin was just leaving."

There was, Tusk felt, some tension in the air. He took a couple of steps, and Martin rose, putting out a pudgy hand almost reluctantly. Martin was not fat, but he gave the appearance of it at first. He was a short man with almost no neck, his large head seemingly connected directly to his shoulders. His face was round and from a distance he gave the impression of a youngish man, not more than forty. But close to, Tusk noticed his jowls and upped the estimate by ten years.

"I just came by to tell Mrs. Pitt how sorry we are about her husband's unfortunate accident," Martin said. "All of us." He chuckled. "We had our differences, but it was a terrible thing."

"Thank you," Anna said. "It was kind of you to stop by." She did not try to hide her eagerness to escort Martin to the door, closed it behind him, turned to face Tusk with a sigh.

"Sorry to bust in like this," he said.

"I'm glad you came," she said. "I don't think I could have stood any more of his condolences." When she walked there was no unnecessary movement. Her legs were long and graceful, the shorts shaped lovingly around her. "I can use a drink."

"Who is Mr. Martin?" Tusk asked as he followed her to the kitchen.

"He's some sort of union officer," she replied.

"He said something about him and Frank having differences."

She handed him his drink. "Frank didn't like him."

She opened the sliding door leading to the patio.

"Why didn't he?" Tusk asked, taking a deck chair facing her. She crossed one leg over the other, sipped her drink.

"Just before...." She paused, took a deep breath and attacked it again. "Just before he was killed he had a run-in with Martin. Martin wanted some kind of payoff or he said he'd start a wobble."

"Wobble?"

"A walkout. Frank told him to go ahead and call his union out, but he wouldn't get another cent."

"I think Frank must have been good at his job," Tusk said.

"He was. It's a small world, nuclear engineering. It's like a large but nosy family. Everyone in the business knows of everyone else. The good ones are in great demand. Frank was building a very good reputation. I sometimes felt he took things a bit too seriously, but I admired him. He said that when sloppy work or excessive government regulation delayed completion of a plant, the loss came out of his pocket, because he had to pay for electricity. He said he had to live near nuclear plants, and someday his children would probably live near them. If it wasn't right he black-marked it, had it done over."

"Sounds like Frank," Tusk said.

"I tried to tell him to slow down, not to be the last of the idealists, to accept the world as it was, and he said he couldn't. I think the pressures were getting to him in the last months." She paused. "How was Mandy?"

"Full of fire," he said. "She sends her love."

"She's a dear."

The late-afternoon sun was losing its heat. It was pleasant on the patio, in the shade of the house. Behind the house the barren rocky hill was taking on a shade of brownish gold. Lindy was silent for long moments.

"Pretty here, in a stark sort of way," Tusk said. "I think I could relate to this country."

She shrugged.

"I'm thinking seriously about staying on for a while," he said.

She returned her eyes to his face quickly.

"I've been kicking around in the camper for a while," he said. "Long time between work. I have the military retirement, of course, but you know how far that goes these days. They say there's plenty of work out at Sweetwater."

"Would it be presumptuous of me to say that you don't have to stay on my account?" she asked, her face serious.

"Not at all. I'll admit that's a part of it. As I said before, you might need a strong back."

"Well," she said, "you didn't call, so I don't have that soupy chicken dish ready."

"Know of a place that serves a decent steak?"

"Thanks," she said, "but I'd planned soup and salad. I'm on nights this week. I'll need a nap before going in at eleven."

"Some other time?"

"Sure," she said, rising as he stood. "Another drink?"

"No, I'll let you get to your soup and salad."

"There's enough for two."

"Some other time," he said.

5

NEWLY CONSTRUCTED ROADS approached the Sweetwater site. At midmorning, traffic was not overly heavy. A brisk wind coming down into the basin off the hills caused the van to sway. He was driving slowly, noting the sprawling new installations along the highway, some of them labeled with the names of giant corporations doing business in the energy field, some of them totally unlabeled. Off to the right he saw the dome of an old reactor. He'd done some homework while waiting for his union card.

The site sprawled across miles of sagebrush flats bounded by a river on one side and a mountain on the other. Nuclear reactors had been in operation there since the days of World War II. Government reactors lined the river, some, of the primitive graphite-core type, no longer in use. A combination of government projects and private industry had made the Sweetwater site the largest nuclear industrial park in the world.

Across the flatness he could see the latest government project, the experimental fast-flux, or

breeder, reactor. To the right was the impressive
Public Power System site, where no fewer than
four boiling-water reactors were under construction. Ahead, nearer the river but still miles from
the line of old government reactors, was his destination: the Tristate Power System reactor
known as Tips.

Oscar, back in the East, had done well, coming
up with a union card and paving a path for him to
one of the one-hundred-forty-plus individual
contractors who were involved in the Tips project. He parked at some distance from the gate,
showed his union card and his personal identification, and announced to the uniformed guard
that, yes, he did have an appointment. He was
given a visitor's badge and escorted to a construction shed that was made to seem tiny by the
bulk of the reactor building rising five-hundred-
plus feet into the dry hot air.

He walked purposefully, briskly, glancing
around to try to familiarize himself with the lay-
out of the ground level, walked past wooden construction barriers, took turns, entered a huge
open area where the sounds of construction
bounced around, saw the tall containment vessel
and, looking up, walked toward it. The size of it
awed him, seemed to draw him. He was careful,
however, not to enter the roped-off space directly under the open equipment bays. He could see
upward for a long way, knew, with a little
prickle of something at the back of his neck, that

the cement surface out there near the containment vessel had received the impact of Frank
Pitt's falling body.

"Excuse me, sir," a female voice said. "May I
ask where is your guide?"

He turned. A solidly built woman in uniform
faced him, expression serious.

"He was here a moment ago," he said.

"It's against the rules to be here without a
guide," the guard said.

"Tell you what," Tusk responded with a grin.
"If you'll show me the way out of this maze I'll
go quietly."

"Yes, sir," she said.

He went home to find Anna Larch had left a
note on his door. Using Anna's phone he called
the number, recognizing it as Lindy's. The Mo-
roccan chicken was bubbling in the pot and she
had some people she wanted him to meet. He
dressed in white ducks and cotton pullover, after
bathing away the heat of the day and the dust of
the construction site and soaking his stumps in a
brine solution, and arrived at Lindy's house just
past seven. Hearing the sound of childish voices
from the backyard, he walked around the house,
opened the gate in the wooden fence. Two small
girls were chasing a ball on the lawn. Lindy was
on the patio with a cheerful-looking woman in
shorts and a man who, upon standing to be intro-
duced, could look Tusk squarely in the eye.

"So we meet the famous Tusk at last," Leigh

Warren said, first to take his hand, looking up from merry brown eyes. Bob Warren's handclasp was firm and quick. Drinks were handy. The sun was low so that it was pleasant outside. The two little girls came over to inspect him curiously and to tell him about their dog being hit by a car and going to the hospital. Lindy looked good in shorts and a blouse tied at the waist to show a sun-browned midriff. It was her night off.

"Understand you're working out at the site," Bob Warren said, having done bartender duty.

"Starting tomorrow morning," Tusk answered.

"I didn't know you were in the field," Leigh said.

"I'm not, really. I'm a wood butcher." He caught a curious look from Bob Warren. "Among other things," he said with a laugh.

"I think he works only when he has to," Lindy explained.

"Lucky lad," Warren said.

"Don't you start complaining," Leigh told him.

"No medical bills," Bob said. "No kiddies' shoes. No house. No bills."

"Anytime you get tired of it, buster," Leigh said, but Tusk could feel a warmth between them, recognized it as prattle talk.

Bob and Leigh were old friends, having met Lindy and Frank on the job at Crystal River, in Florida. When the women went inside to see to the meal, Bob Warren refilled their glasses. "Old Frank told me about that boat ride he took you on in Nam."

"Damned fool almost got me killed," Tusk said.

"They asked me to volunteer for that river work," Bob said.

"I take it you didn't."

"Bet your sweet ass I didn't. I liked it little enough right there where I was."

"Where was that?"

"Out in the gulf, mostly. Guided-missile destroyer."

"Not the same one Frank was on?"

"No. But doing about the same thing Frank did. Like him, I got my first nuclear training in the navy. Came out and went to tech school and started out as a technician, just like he did."

"I don't know all there is to know about what Frank did," Tusk said.

"He was in start-up. Coming out here was a step up for him, just as it was for me. We were executives." He laughed. "Which meant we didn't work with tools anymore, and sometimes I'm sorry. Frank had a section of the job for which he was responsible. He was sort of a glorified foreman, except that he knew his job. Made it a point to know all there was to know, was always learning, looking into other sections that were not his responsibility. It got to the point where when the NRC came around—"

"I don't know the language, either," Tusk said.

"Nuclear Regulatory Commission. They have periodic inspections. It's a real tear-ass thing and scares most people. They can be tough. But since

Frank knew all there was to know about the whole plant it got to the point where he was given the job of going around with the NRC, and he'd get just as nervous as anyone else and expect it to be a twelve-hour ordeal, and he knew his stuff so well that he could do in four hours what usually took ten or twelve."

"So you're a start-up engineer?" Tusk asked.

"That's what we're called. We're the guys who get the reactor built—get it started up. We're not real engineers. At least most of us, are like me and Frank. Tech-school diploma. No degree. But it's a funny business. Things move so fast, technology advances so quickly, that the only way you can learn the job is to do it. You take a kid just out of a seven-year course with a bright new degree that says he's a real engineer, and they send him to men like us to train. It hurts a little, knowing he's starting at more than you're making, that when you teach him the facts of life he'll be put in charge over you."

"Yeah, I can see where that would make Frank a little angry," Tusk said.

"I used to tell him that he took things a little too seriously," Bob said. "I'd say, 'Hey, boy, take it easy. Let someone else do the worrying; you're not getting paid to worry.' But he did. He'd raise hell and get the brass all rattled."

"Sounds like him."

"We've got this horse's behind as a supervisor," Bob said. "Boss of the whole start-up section. About as much business being in a nuclear plant as a baboon in the cockpit of a jet fighter. But this is a state operation, civil service, seniority, all that jazz. Frank told him to his face that he was going to do everything he could to get him fired.''

"How to win friends and influence people,'' Tusk commented wryly.

He had a feeling that Bob Warren would be good at his job, too. There was, under an exterior of relaxed ease, a certain tightness. All the good ones, in any field, seemed to have it: a reserve of readiness, an awareness.

"Tips is an old company, and it looks after its own,'' Bob went on. "This man, Johnson, the supervisor, isn't too far from retirement. He's reached the highest point he'll ever reach in this job, and if it's ever finished he'll be pushed back into an office somewhere and forgotten until he's given his gold watch. Meanwhile he's hanging on with all his teeth, and the company, knowing that he isn't qualified for the job, just lets him occupy space waiting for the big day. I can live with him, because I just go on and do my job and then tell him what I've done, but Frank didn't operate that way. I told him he was doing himself out of the promotion he deserved by rattling Abe Johnson's cage all the time. Sure enough, he was passed over. They put a kid just out of school in the job Frank was up for.''

Everything he had heard fit with Frank's character. Frank had always been perhaps a bit too intense, too much of the perfectionist. He had pushed himself in everything he did. Take the patrol boat in Nam. Others ran the channel out in the center, hauling ass, trying to avoid trouble. Frank went slow and easy, exploring close in, looking for Cong. "We're here to clear up the river," he'd told Tusk, "not just joyride."

Interesting, hearing people talk about him. He had met only two people who'd worked with Frank, a co-worker who'd liked him and a union official who'd had his differences with him, but he was beginning to get a picture. There was not, of course, anything in what he'd heard to support his deeply felt belief that Frank had not merely stumbled over the edge and plunged five hundred feet to a cement floor, but there were at least two people at the site who'd had reason to dislike him.

"It was quite a shock when I heard what had happened," he said. "I still can't picture Frank standing close enough to the edge of a drop to fall over."

"Over a guardrail," Bob Warren added, nodding.

"Did something to do with his job take him up there?"

"That area wasn't in his section," Bob said. "But as I've said, he took it upon himself to know every section. If any one man could explain the whole vast, complicated mess, it was

Frank. I don't know. We were planning to knock off early that day. We were in the office and he got a phone call. He told me to go on out and he'd meet me in the parking lot. We rode to work together, you know. I cleaned up some details and walked on outside. I was standing outside the plant when it happened.''

"He had a phone call?" Tusk asked.

"He didn't say who. He just said he had to go see someone.''

"No indication as to whom?"

"I'm trying to remember his exact words,'' Bob said. "He picked up the phone, said 'Pitt,' listened for a minute and said, 'Yeah, okay.' Then he told me to wait for him outside, that he had to go see a man about a dog.''

Tusk knew the phrase. If you had private business and someone asked you where you were going, you said, "I'm going to see a man about a dog." So someone had called, and it was pertaining to something private, and the meeting place had been top level, and then Frank had gone tumbling down five hundred feet.

He was musing over it when the women came out, a big steaming kettle being carried by Lindy, Leigh Warren laden with a covered dish containing a very good bread. The meal was simple, chicken poached in a liquid flavored with spices, lemon, almonds, tomatoes. The two little girls received a lot of attention until they finished their meal and were taken off to watch TV in the house. It took only one question from Tusk to turn the talk once again to the nuclear industry. Leigh and Lindy were as interested in talking about it as Bob.

Aside from some crash reading in the past couple of days, Tusk's knowledge of the nuclear industry and its ramifications was limited to what he'd read in newspapers and seen on national news.

"Tell me about radiation," he said.

"Well, there's a lot to know, and here's an example. The papers and TV made a big deal about TMI venting some krypton into the air when they started opening up the containment building. You could have put a counter to the face of a watch with a dial that glows in the dark and got a higher reading. Usually when we talk about radiation we're talking about very small amounts, millirems, thousandths of rems. It takes about twenty-five rems before you begin to have any blood-cell damage. And that's all at once."

"I think people are afraid of it because you can't see it," Tusk said.

"Look, if there were any way we could have the power we need without nuclear reactors, I'd be all for it," Bob said. "It's mean stuff, and even if you do get more radiation skiing on a high mountain than you do working in a nuclear plant, I don't ski on high mountains. I don't expose my body to the good old sun, either, because we know the sun causes skin cancer. But I don't see how we're going to maintain any kind of standard of living without nuclear energy. I'm not willing to go back to living in a cave and watching television by candlelight. We probably will lose lives sooner or later, because you can't eliminate the human element from it, and when something bad happens it'll most likely be through human error. We may not be able to build a bridge that won't fall down, or a building that won't collapse on a crowd inside, but we have developed nuclear reactors under the most stringent safeguards in the history of industry.''

"What I can't understand," Lindy said, "is the so-called environmentalists who march against any nuclear plant and talk about the dangers and how a plant ruins the sacred environment, but they talk about solar as if it were a religion and wouldn't hesitate to cover half of Arizona with solar panels.''

"And what would all that concentrated ultraviolet do to the workers?" Leigh asked.

"I'm not quite that old," Tusk said, "but I know that in World War II we designed and built the B-29, a very complicated weapons system, in about two years, and they say it's going to take decades to do anything about the energy situation.''

"Government controls," Bob said. "Safety regulations. Unions. Astronomical costs. The B-29 was a wartime project, money no object. Now Big Brother is looking after us all so closely that a five-mile-an-hour bumper that isn't safe at five miles adds hundreds of dollars to the price of an automobile. To keep some idiot from buying a piece of Florida swamp by mail, federal regulations have added thousands to the cost of a house. Multiply that by millions and you have the nuclear industry.''

"I'm in a nest of conservatives,'' Tusk laughed.

It was a pleasant evening, and it was Tusk who ended it, saying that he had to hit the sack because he was going to his first day of work the next morning. As he left, Bob Warren shook his hand and said to give him a call if he needed any help. Tusk had a feeling he'd be seeing more of the friendly engineer, but he was surprised when, after reporting to his foreman and being sent to the front of the reactor building to join a crew assigned to some off-site work, he saw Bob Warren, in faded jeans and T-shirt, hard hat pushed back, standing beside a pickup truck.

"Hear you need a carpenter," he said.

"Small world,'' said Bob. "Toss the tools in the back.''

Tusk went off to the job—a protective railing was needed for some pipe fitters. At the end of the shift the other workers disappeared. Warren motioned for Tusk to follow him into the reactor. He led the way into a large room partitioned off into tiny cubicles, two desks in each cubicle, the partitions at chest height.

"I just have to take care of a few things,'' he

said. "It won't take long, so stick around. I've got to see a man about a union. There's coffee over there."

He sat in Bob's little cubicle of an office for a few minutes. From the conversation of the night before, he knew that Bob had shared the office with Frank before his death. The other desk, in contrast to Bob's was a model of neatness, papers tucked carefully in wire baskets, ashtray clean. A lower drawer of the desk had been locked with a hasp and padlock, a combination lock.

The swinging door of the cubicle opened. Tusk looked up to see a neatly dressed young man, slacks unwrinkled, white shirt turned up at the cuffs, unsoiled, tie loosened at the neck.

"Hi," the newcomer said. "Can I help you?"

"I'm waiting for Bob Warren. He's gone off on some union business."

"Oh, I see. I'm Mark Lingate."

Tusk started to rise, but Lingate stepped past his feet, pulled out his chair, sat down, his manner telling Tusk that he didn't care who the hell Tusk was. Tusk was silent. In profile Lingate was strong, with a good chin, a straight nose, and hair, as he removed his hard hat, that was black and curling, moderately long. He had the look, Tusk thought, of a young man on the way up, a man with ambition, always neat, always polite to those who were superior to him.

It was a small cubicle, and as Lingate began pulling papers from a wire basket, Tusk stood up. "Think I'll have some coffee. Want some?"

"Thanks, just cream," Lingate said, as if it were his due to be served.

The coffee had been simmering in a metal brewer until it was dark and acidy and chewy. The Styrofoam cups were beginning to make heat felt on the tips of his fingers before he made it back to the little office. Lingate was leaning back in his chair.

"What happened out there?" Lingate asked, taking his coffee without thanks.

"Just exercising a union contract," Tusk said.

"If Bob's mixing in with the union he's going to get his tail caught in a grinder, just like Pitt," Lingate said.

"Pitt?" Tusk asked innocently. No need to let it be known that he knew Frank.

"He's the one killed in the accident. This was his desk." He smiled. His lips were the sort that some women find sensual, but to Tusk he looked just a bit too pretty. "It was a bad deal, but as the old saying goes, there is some good in all bad. At least I have a place to sit down now."

He covered the instinctive beginning of attack, the urge to maul the bastard, by making his lunge forward into a leg-scratching motion. He controlled his quick anger as Bob Warren came into the cubicle. Three men crowded it. Warren's face was grim.

"Bad?" Lingate asked.

"The usual crap," Warren growled. He waved

a hand at Tusk. "Smith's a carpenter. I thought we'd get him to take that lock off."

"Bless you," said Lingate.

"Wanna take a look, Smith?" Bob asked. His voice was formal, a superior speaking to a worker. "Man had the desk before Mark put it on. Mr. Johnson is afraid we're going to damage the valuable desk if we rip it off." The use of his last name hadn't escaped Tusk. Well, maybe Warren was just professional in his approach to his job. Tusk knelt, examined the hasp and lock. The hasp screws were, of course, covered by the hinge of the hasp.

"Have to pry out the screws," he said. "It'll leave holes, but to protect the integrity of this fine piece of furniture, I can fill them with putty."

"Whatever," Lingate said.

"Won't take long," Tusk said. "I can go get a screwdriver and do it right now."

"No, that's okay," Lingate said. "Tomorrow's soon enough."

"Fine. One of you speak to my foreman?"

"I'll do that," Warren offered. "Now I'm going to hit the gate."

Tusk made his way to the construction shed, punched out, stored his tools in the locker assigned to him. He was in no hurry, took his time walking across the compound, out the gate. He saw Bob Warren standing beside his four-wheeler in the parking lot. He was leaning on a fender, feet crossed, a cigarette in his hand.

"I wanna be there when you open that drawer," he said.

"You're the boss." Tusk remembered how formal Warren had been in the presence of Mark Lingate.

"There's a lot of things wrong with this plant," said Bob. "A couple of crooked union bosses are holding out for a payoff. They're making their unions work slow to get their point across. Frank was after their asses. But he was a careful man. He worked slow and he got things documented—down on paper. I took lessons. I just went in to my boss with all the figures. Strikes cost money but if we pay up to those guys they'll never stop demanding more. My boss agreed with me. 'Warren,' he said, 'you keep on the way you're going and I'll handle the flak.' "

"Umm," Tusk said.

"There's a beer joint down the road. It's usually safe enough. Come on, I'll buy you one."

Tusk shrugged. He followed the four-wheeler out of the lot, parked behind it at the beer joint, on the outskirts of Petertown. A sign said, No Checks Accepted Here. There was one advantage to being in the West, in an area where there were Hispanic farm workers. The bar had Dos Equis. Cold and good. Beers in hand, the two men took a booth at the back. It smelled of old beer and cigars.

"Hope you understood my pulling the me-boss-you-worker gig in front of Lingate," Bob said.

"No sweat."

"I figure the fewer people know why you're here the better," he said, looking Tusk straight in the eye.

"I don't know what you're thinking," Tusk said. "I'm here by accident. I stopped by to see an old friend, and he was dead. I figured his wife might need some moral support, and I need to work a little because I was getting low."

"Sure," Bob said. "But we both know that Frank didn't fall all by himself, don't we?"

Tusk shrugged, drank the good Mexican beer from the bottle.

"Look, take your time on that drawer tomorrow morning. I'll have to be out and around early, but I'll try to get back around ten. Frank was the only one who had the combination to that lock, and it's been closed since he died. I'd like to see what's inside."

"Wouldn't Lindy be the one to say who should see Frank's personal papers?" Tusk asked.

"Hey, come on. We were both friends of Frank's."

Tusk nodded. He was not overly concerned that Warren suspected he was anything but a construction bum.

As if reading his thoughts, Warren grinned. "You're not just a union carpenter, Tusk. You're far too inquisitive for that."

6

"You go up to start-up," the foreman told him next morning. "See Bob Warren."

He was beginning to know the first two levels of the maze that was the reactor building. He made his way up the stairs, the elevator being much in use first thing in the morning. The cubicle was empty. It took him about two minutes to drive the blade of a large screwdriver under the hasp, apply pressure, rip the screws out of the old wood.

At first the contents of the drawer were disappointing. It was packed to the top, however, and under a stack of technical manuals, folded plans of various parts of the plant, were half a dozen spiral notebooks.

He opened the first. It was dated in the past year, a few days after Frank had come to work at Tips. In Frank's hurried scrawl there was detailed a technical problem involving steam pipes, part of a safety system, that ran outside the plant.

"Told Johnson, and the NRC, that the pipes

were inadequate," Frank had written. "Told them that changing them now would be cheaper than changing them in future."

It was all technical, dealing with problems faced by a man who was interested in his job. A hint of dissatisfaction had begun to creep in after Frank was on the job for only three months. Inserted into the notebook were four neatly typed pages. The gist of it was that Johnson had given the wrong specs to a contractor.

"I called the mistake to the attention of Mr. Johnson," Frank wrote. "I was told to mind my own business. Since the faulty installation was in my section, I considered it to be my business. I pointed out the specific NRC regulations to Mr. Johnson and, failing to convince him, went over his head."

There followed a description of the project, which Tusk skipped. At the end of the report, which Tusk guessed had been submitted to higher authority, an inked note stated that the installation had been dismantled and was now being installed properly.

An entire section of the second notebook detailed bad decisions made by Abe Johnson, start-up supervisor. Another section was a detailed accounting of misconduct by some of the men, man-hours lost, cost to the utility.

It was in the last book that Tusk found the piece of brown paper bag. It was inserted near the back of the notebook where Frank's careful documentation of his actions and decisions ended. In crude block letters someone had printed, EASE UP, SMART-ASS, OR. . . . Below was a stickman, his head being cut off by a crudely drawn welder's torch.

He put the piece of brown paper in his wallet, began to read the entries for the last months of Frank's life, met Mark Lingate there, a graduate engineer, holding the equivalent of a master's degree, being trained by Frank. Frank's opinion was that Lingate was a nice enough kid, sharp with a slide rule or a computer but, like all college men, without practical experience.

He felt a prickle at the back of his neck as he neared the last entries and read, "Inspecting welds on level four, was almost struck by a bundle of welding rods. Missed my head by inches. Heavy enough to do me in. Went up the scaffolding in a hurry—" the adrenal gland must have been pumping, Tusk thought, to send him climbing up scaffolding "—but no one there. The rods could have fallen by themselves after being left in a bad position. I asked around and no one had seen anyone there. Bardoni's crew was on that section, but off on a break at the time."

Alerted to Bardoni, Frank had done a study of the crew headed by him. In Frank's opinion, Angelo Bardoni was a complete deadhead, his crew doing less work and making more bad welds than any other crew.

At times, the notes took on the form of a semi-journal, with personal observations inserted. "Feel like hell after the party at Bob's," was an example. Also recorded were calls from other firms in the industry who had contacted him to talk to him about changing jobs. Reminders, too, indicating that he had read through his material often. "Invite Johnny and his wife, Fred, Mark to the cookout Friday."

But mainly it was an insurance policy, Frank's notes, a detailed account of his work, his decisions, his reasons for making decisions. More than once there were typed pages inserted with figures and crisply written explanations, indicating that he'd had to justify something to someone higher up.

Tusk was especially alert to the names that Frank mentioned, and there were several that he encountered quite often. Bob Warren, co-worker and friend; the supervisor; Lingate, the young graduate engineer; "Stu," apparently also an engineer working under Frank; and several times the name of the union leader whom Tusk had encountered at the Pitt house, mostly in the context of conferences to iron out some dispute with the pipe-fitters union, Martin being the union's spokesman. But toward the end there was an entry that caught Tusk's full attention. It was brief and it had words underlined.

It consisted of four words. "*Get* Martin's ass *tomorrow.*"

The entry was dated the day before Frank's

death, and Tusk could almost see the satisfied grin on Frank's face as he scrawled the sentence. He was musing over it, for it could be significant or it could be merely another indication of the continuing hassle with management, when the swinging door banged and Bob Warren came in.

"I thought you were going to wait for me," Warren said.

"I just got it open," Tusk answered.

He made no objection as Bob stood beside him and started going through the stack of manuals and blueprints, picked up a notebook and sat down at his desk, began to read.

"Dynamite," he said after a while. "He's got old Johnson nailed to the wall."

Tusk lighted a cigarette and waited as Warren scanned, flipping pages rapidly.

"I'd like to go over these a little closer sometime," Warren said.

"I'm sure Lindy won't object." Tusk rose, gathered up all the material, put it in his toolbox. "Did Frank mention a near accident to you?"

"The welding rods falling? Yeah, he told me. He didn't seem to be too concerned. You have to watch your head around here. Things like that happen all the time. We haven't killed anyone with radiation yet, but we do have our share of the normal construction accidents, if you can call an accident normal."

"Did Frank seem unusually tense to you in the last days?"

"Well, he was wound pretty tight. Management's putting on the pressure because we're so far behind. It's like the military chain of command, you know. The general gets pissed and he chews the colonel and it comes down at last to the buck private in the rear rank. Then, too, he had a decision to make."

"About what?"

"He'd had a good offer from one of the body shops."

"Translate," Tusk said.

"A consulting firm. It works this way. You go to work as a tech, learn about the hardware by installing it and repairing it, then when you know the job you move up to start-up and tell others how to do it. Just as you begin to be worth something to the utility one of the consulting firms comes along and offers more money. They contract their experience and services to utilities with problems, like at TMI, or during construction. The advantage is you're out of the hassle, mostly. You're under contract to the body shop, so you don't have to take any crap from men like Abe Johnson."

"Did Frank want to leave?"

"Hell, we all want to leave if we can find a better job. Frank wasn't sure. He was mad because he'd been promised a promotion and didn't get it, but he also hoped he could get Abe Johnson's job when Johnson retired. He was having a lot of trouble making up his mind. He liked his house and the country, the desert and the mountains and all, and this offer he had was going to take him back East into the big cities.''

"Did he talk to you about his troubles with Ernest Martin?''

"Bet your sweet ass. Everyone has trouble with him. He's one of the guys I was telling you about.''

"Any particular trouble with Martin that you remember?''

"No, just the usual. He made trouble, Frank made trouble, he made trouble back.''

"Well, I guess I'll fill up these holes in the desk and get back to the shack,'' Tusk said. He selected putty of almost the right color and spread it on with a putty knife.

"What about that crew pusher he mentioned—Bardoni?'' Tusk asked.

"He's a gold-plated bastard,'' Bob said. "Plain mean.''

"Do carpenters ever work with a pipe-fitting crew?''

"Sure. Scaffolding, temporary partitions, things like that.''

"Could you fix it for me to work with Bardoni?''

"Probably. You know about his fight with Frank, huh?''

"No. Tell me.''

"It came after the big NRC inspection when Frank black-lined all the bad welds. Bardoni said he was just being chicken-shit about it, and Frank unloaded on him, telling him that he was a sorry excuse for a pipe fitter. It was one helluva fight, boy. Bardoni's a big bastard, and it'd be hard to say who won.''

"Bardoni the kind to hold a grudge?''

Warren shrugged. "I don't think he has the intelligence to hold a grudge. He's the kind who enjoys a good fight, even if he does get cut up a little. They shook hands afterward, both of them sitting on the floor with blood all over. That didn't make Frank like Bardoni. He rode him pretty hard, told him he was going to have to start doing acceptable work. He said he was going to lodge a formal complaint to the union, but I don't think he got around to it.''

"Could that have been why he was going to see Martin the day he was killed?''

"I don't know. He was a little bit moody that morning on the way to work. I asked him who had licked the red off his candy, and he just shrugged.''

"I haven't had a chance to see this place yet,'' Tusk said. "Think you could give me a guided tour?''

"Why not?'' Warren rose and took off at a lope, his long-legged strides causing Tusk to sling his feet a bit faster than usual. He blew a kiss toward the girl at the reception desk, told her where he'd be in case he was needed, fingered the paging device fastened to his belt and took off. They stood in line for an elevator, entered with a crew pushing portable equipment, stood silently amid the rank aroma of sweat and cigarettes as the elevator, scarcely an express, stopped at almost every level.

When Bob led the way out they were at the top, the dome of the containment building overhead, the reactor vessel itself—a huge and somehow grim-looking presence, a portion of it at the top level draped with the protecting plastic sheets, torches and welding arcs sizzling behind the plastic. The floor extended around the reactor vessel, barren except for equipment and stores stacked against the outer walls. The equipment bay was open, protected by a rail of firmly implanted two-inch pipe.

"It happened here," Bob said.

Tusk walked to the rail, put his hands on it, felt his knuckles go tense and white as he looked down, down, along the curved reactor vessel, five hundred feet, and the men below, at ground level, were midgets. Aside from the pipe fitters behind their almost opaque screening, the top level was deserted. He could have shoved Bob Warren over, disappeared into the maze of stairwells, levels, corridors, and no one would have ever known if instead of leaving the start-up office with Bob he had called him to meet him on the top.

He had leaped from an aircraft at a height equal to that five hundred feet, and had time for his chute to deploy, open and deposit him on the ground. It was a long, long way down, and even to a man who was not afraid of heights, who would step out the door of an aircraft and fall free for a full minute before opening his chute, looking down that shaft to the cold hard cement was unpleasant. For a man like Frank, with an almost psychopathic fear of heights, the moments would have been sheer terror.

Bob Warren respected his mood, stood to one side and behind.

He had never told Frank goodbye, and did it then, looking down, envisioning what was left of Frank's body. He'd seen a man plow in during training at Ft. Bragg, both chutes, main and reserve, streaming uselessly above him, saw legs accordioned, bones splintered, thighs driven out of sockets, intestines ruptured, purple and glossy. So he said his goodbyes to a boy who'd once hunted rabbits with him, later on joined in the girl hunt with him, wept with him when they bombed out and lost the state championship by one lousy point.

They went down level by level, Bob acting as tour guide, through an amazing complex of endless, convoluted, overlapping piping of sizes large enough for a man to crawl through.

Tusk tried to concentrate, found himself hopelessly lost. Questions told him that the outside stairwells gave access; that he could, if the occasion arose and he didn't want to use the elevator, make his way topside on the outside wells.

The control room had some equipment installed, complicated pinball boards of lights and switches and buttons in plastic cocoons, raised floor, mazes of electrical boxes standing higher than his head, a worm's nightmare of wiring inside an opened box, a system so vastly complicated, so technical, so extensive, that it seemed impossible for any one man to understand it. In simple terms, a boiling-water reactor used the heat of atomic disintegration to boil water into steam, and the steam then used its power, the power of intense pressure, to turn the huge turbines. But nothing was simple, the entire process complicated by the deadly radioactivity that, along with heat, came from the core of the reactor, requiring complicated systems for reclaiming the slightly radioactive steam, cooling it back to liquid stage, reusing it, reheating it, all systems duplicated, safety insured to the limit of man's ingenuity by multiple fail-safes and expensive redundancy of features, and huge vessels in the cooling section.

"I've seen 'em bounce up and down like a runaway train," Bob said. And after looking briefly into a maze of pipes, selecting a weld that showed irregularity, "Here's a problem," he said. "A good weld is flowed on all in one operation, making it solid and uniform. This man either didn't know his business or was thinking about getting off and having a cold one. Tried to cover up by adding another layer. So underneath you've got a bad weld, and under pressure the superheated steam finds a tiny pinhole, the weld layers separate, and the whole thing shuts down at the cost of thousands of dollars and maybe some radioactive steam in the containment. That's the kind of thing Frank couldn't stand."

A bit stunned, awed by the size, the complexity, Tusk followed Bob Warren's lope, asked his questions, tried to remember the circuitous pathway down from the top. Now and then, as they passed workers, mostly not working, smoking, leaning, sitting, drinking coffee, a man would speak, one calling out, "How's it going, Big Bob?"

Bob had friendly words for all of them, said in an aside, "See why we're years behind? Why the cost override alone is more than the original estimated cost?"

At lunchtime Tusk took Frank Pitt's papers and locked them in a little cabinet he'd built under the bunk in the van. A determined man could find it if he looked hard enough, but the van didn't look prosperous enough to get a thorough going-over by a pro, the biggest danger being that it might be taken, all of it, by some amateur who knew enough to break a window and hot-wire it. In the little cabinet was a stash of spare cash, a couple of sets of identification, and two guns, a palm-sized .32 automatic and the old dependable

G.I. .45, both guaranteed to be totally and completely untraceable.

He spent the afternoon lounging around the construction shack, on full pay, no assignment available. He clocked out early, drove to his room, passed the time of day with Anna Larch while declining to share a bologna sandwich for dinner, and spent the early evening going over Frank's notes with great care. As Bob Warren had said, Frank was a careful man. Before he bucked, he was sure of his ground, had the facts on paper. And if every big construction site in the country suffered as much from greed, ignorance and stupidity as this one, the country was in one helluva fix.

7

"I HOPE YOU HAVEN'T EATEN," Belinda Pitt said. She had a nice telephone voice.

"I was going out to take advantage of modern civilization," Tusk replied. "A Big Mac."

"Bob and Leigh just called," she said. "He's offered to rescue you from Big Macs and French fries. Can you pick me up in, oh, a half hour or so?"

He had been seeking an excuse to see her. He wasn't quite ready to lay the whole picture on her, show her Frank's notebooks and the little piece of brown paper with the threat; and the dinner invitation from the Warrens served its purpose. He pulled the van in behind the Scout in the driveway. She saw him come up, was walking down the path before he could get out. She wore white slacks and a pretty little flowered blouse, her flaxen hair pulled back. She had, he decided, a model's walk, but without the emotive overstatement. He held the door, took her arm and helped her into the van.

Not knowing how long he'd have, as she gave

him directions, he got to it immediately. "Did you know that Frank was thinking of changing jobs?"

"Yes. He talked things over with me. It seemed to give him an outlet. He'd come home from the job all tensed up and I'd give him about thirty minutes. He'd putter around, maybe empty the garbage or something, and then he'd come into the living room for his drink and tell me about his day. We had no secrets."

"Apparently he was no favorite of Abe Johnson's," he said.

"Take the next right," she said. "Frank was, in a way, a hard man. He had no patience with incompetence. Made no bones about stating his opinions. I'm sure if Johnson would have found an excuse he'd have sacked him."

"Just how serious were Frank's problems with Ernest Martin?"

"Oh, he was always having problems with him. When he black-lined so many welds that time, it was Martin who came to discuss it. Had a big meeting. I don't know if Martin had anything to do with it, but he had a fight with a pipe fitter."

"Man named Bardoni?" Tusk asked.

"You do get around quickly, don't you?" she asked. "One day on the job and you're up to date on everything."

"Not quite everything. Why the fight?" He grinned. "And who won?"

"I asked him how the other fellow looked,"

she said. "He wasn't pretty. He wore a shiner for weeks. Why? I guess it just got to be too much for him and he had to hit someone."

"He started it?"

"No, not exactly. At least, he didn't throw the first punch."

"Lindy, would you say that Frank's troubles on this job were normal or worse than normal?"

"Worse, I'd say. Of course, this was the first position in which he had any real responsibility. But there just seemed to be more trouble than there'd been in Florida or in Maine." She mused for a moment. "It seemed to eat at him, this job."

"Don't think I'm being disloyal when I ask this," Tusk said, "but could it be that he was just in over his head, taking on a job he wasn't quite ready for?"

"No. I was afraid of that at first, and he worried about it, too. But he was good. He had about one job offer every two weeks. People called him from Ohio, North Carolina, Idaho. All over. He was just waiting for the right one. Word gets around in this business. If he hadn't been good, they wouldn't have been after him."

"So why was he so uptight?" Tusk asked, glancing at her. "He took out a ten-thousand-dollar insurance policy in Mandy's name. A man in his thirties buying a policy with a seventy-five-year-old woman as beneficiary?"

She thought about that one for a moment, told

him to take a left, looked out of the window. "I don't know," she said at last.

"No special reason for his suddenly feeling his mortality?"

A tear made a damp track down her cheek. She brushed it away with the back of her hand. "No."

The Warrens lived in a stone-and-stained-paneling house in a new development that climbed the side of a sagebrush hill. Back in North Carolina Tusk's partners in a land-development plan were building half a dozen houses that were larger, better designed and sold for as much as twenty thousand less. But it was a solidly designed house nevertheless, a bit un-imaginative, surrounded by a perfect lawn, the backyard fenced.

"They'll be in back," Lindy said, leading the way.

The two Warren children were in a king-size swimming pool, paddling on floating duckies, waving and calling out to Lindy as she and Tusk entered the backyard. Leigh Warren came to meet them. "I hope you brought a swimsuit," she said. She wore a semibikini that showed that she was a lot of woman, big hipped, large breasted, and just about five pounds too much for the suit. The effect, however, if not sensual, was wholesome. Bob had on a pair of faded trunks that came halfway down his legs, surfer-1950s style.

"I'm afraid not," Tusk said, although there was a pair of trunks in the van, in one of the closets.

"We're about the same build," Bob said. "I'll fix you up." He went away with his long lope and came back carrying a newer and less faded pair of trunks. "Change in there. Lindy keeps one here all the time."

In fact, Lindy and Leigh had disappeared, and while Bob did the bartender honors they came back, Lindy looking devastating in a dark brown bikini. There are girls and there are girls, and when there is a girl with a lovely long waist, tucked in incredibly small atop outflowing feminine hips, supported by perfectly proportioned legs that are too long to be believed; when breasts stand proudly under skimpy cover and flaxen hair emphasizes a face of spectacular beauty, men look. Tusk found himself frozen, drink halfway to his mouth, staring. Bob whistled.

"Knock it off, buster," Leigh said.

Lindy caught his look before he could recover, and a faint flush crept up her long graceful neck. "You're not dressed for swimming," she said, coming to take Bob's offered drink.

"Too much trouble," Tusk said. "I'll be an appreciative spectator."

"No way," Leigh said. "After what we shelled out for this pool, swimming is mandatory for all guests."

He shrugged, finished his drink, took Bob's trunks and went into the dressing room-bath that had been added to the back of the house. He came out with his feet still strapped in place, not wanting to knee-walk across the flagstone border of the pool, and sat down in a lawn chair.

The older of the little girls surfaced, splashed lustily to the side of the pool and smiled up at him. "Are you going to swim in your shoes?" she asked.

"That would get them all wet, wouldn't it?" he asked.

Little sister joined the older girl clinging to the side of the pool as he bent, undid the straps, removed a foot and set it behind the chair out of splash distance. Two sets of young eyes went wide in wonder. The three adults were at the bar, preparing another round, Lindy coming toward him with two glasses in hand as he removed the other foot and dropped it with a clunk behind the chair.

"Wow," the younger girl said.

"He has no feet," the older one said, looking up wide-eyed as Lindy, smiling, glanced down, began to bend to hand Tusk his drink and froze, her face ashen.

"How can you swim with no feet?" the older girl asked.

"I float a lot," Tusk said, noting Lindy's stricken look. It had not occurred to him that she didn't know. He'd long since stopped being sensitive about it. It had happened, and no amount of wailing about it would alter the fact. But her embarrassment had an effect on him, reminded him that he'd been reluctant to undress and get into the pool. Usually he welcomed any chance to get into the water. That, he told himself in the instant before she recovered and handed him the drink, would bear some self-examination.

"Run along, girls," Lindy said. "Stop bothering Mr. Smith."

Bob and Leigh, laughing, approached, drinks in hand. Bob took it in stride, glancing down, then up to Tusk's face. Leigh cleared her throat.

"Nam?" Bob asked.

"I'll never be accused of having both feet on the ground," Tusk said. He shoved himself down into the water, went under, surfaced and took strong arm strokes toward the other end. The two little girls followed, flailing wildly at the water.

"Boy," the older one said, "you swim good without feet."

"I couldn't do it," said the younger one.

"You could if you didn't have any other choice," Tusk said.

"My dolly lost a foot," the younger one said, "and my mom sewed it back on."

"They tried that with me," Tusk grinned, "and they kept falling off."

"Really?"

He laughed. "Wanna race to the other end?"

"Well," said the older one gravely, "I suppose, to be fair, that we should give you a head start."

"All right, sucker," Tusk said, starting off. He swam just slowly enough for the girls to stay by his side.

"Boy, that was close," the older one panted.

"Tell you what," Tusk said. "Let's play a trick on your father, okay?"

They gathered close, giggling in anticipation. "Let's bet your father that I can beat him in a race."

"But you have no feet."

"We're going to fix that," he whispered. "Look, when they're not looking, you go out front and open the door of my van. Look under the back seat and you'll see a pair of swim fins. You know what I mean?" The older girl nodded, all seriousness. "Sneak them to me and then we'll have the race. Don't let anyone see them."

Vast giggles of conspiracy went on as Tusk swam to the edge of the pool, swung himself up to sit on the side. Warren was talking about delays in building the reactor. Lindy sat in a lawn chair, long lovely legs stretched out in front. She seemed to be listening, but her eyes were not on Bob, were directed upward toward the sky, beginning to take on the deep blue of twilight.

Hiding giggles behind their hands, the two little girls walked with suspicious casualness to the gate and disappeared. For five minutes Lindy did not look at him, did not speak.

"How's your drink?" Tusk asked her, sliding to reach his feet.

Still she did not look. "Fine," she said.

He put the feet on without strapping them, shuffled to the bar. The girls were back, at the gate, standing outside giggling. When Bob came to the bar to check on Tusk's progress with his drink, Tusk saw the girls run in, each carrying a fin, and jump into the pool. He waited only a few minutes before taking off his feet and getting back into the pool himself. He swam to the giggling little girls and took the fins. They were custom-made, legs extending above the muscles of his calves, secured there by a strap with a stainless-steel buckle. He managed to get them on without attracting the attention of the adults.

"You may now issue our challenge," he told the older girl.

"Daddy, come on in," she called.

Bob waved and said, "In a minute."

"We're going to have a race," she said. "Come on."

"Come on," the younger seconded. "Don't be chicken."

"Chicken, is it?" Bob grinned, putting aside his drink. He dived in, surfaced, blowing, and came to stand in the shallow water. "I can beat you two with one hand."

"No," the older one said. "You're going to race Mr. Smith."

Bob gave Tusk a quick look. Tusk, grinning, nodded.

"Well," Bob said, "I don't think Mr. Smith wants to race."

"He does," Tusk said. He grinned at the girls. "I think we should have a bet, don't you, ladies?"

"Yes, yes," they chorused.

"What would be a good bet?" Tusk asked.

"A new bicycle," they said, almost together.

"No deal," Bob said. "What have you got to bet?"

The older one thought seriously. "All right," she said decisively. "If Mr. Smith wins, we get to stay up an hour later."

"And *when* I win?" Bob asked, winking at Tusk.

"If you win we empty the garbage for a week."

"Two weeks," Bob said, holding up two fingers.

The older one looked at Tusk doubtfully. He winked and nodded yes. "All right," she said.

"Four lengths of the pool?" Tusk asked.

"Suit yourself," Bob said.

The girls, serious, tense, helped them into position, pushing, giving instruction. The older one said, "Ready, set, go."

Bob started slowly, not pushing. Tusk dragged his fins and used his arms, falling just a little behind. The girls were yelling excitedly, urging him on. He was behind when Bob turned, lazily, at the end of the pool. He opened up on the way back, using the fins in a swift butterfly, passed Bob before he reached the end of the pool.

"Hey," Bob yelled.

The girls were screaming in excitement. Bob did a racing turn, came out swimming seriously. Tusk flipped at the far end, really stretched it out on the third lap, was roaring down toward the end of the fourth lap just as Bob made his turn at the end of three. He met two yelling, excited little girls, picked them up.

Bob puffed up, stood, panted and grinned. "Now that's called using a handicap to advantage," he said. "And you two conspiring against your own father!"

It had served its purpose, Tusk's little trick. When they were dressed, the steaks sizzling on the grill, Leigh and Bob were relaxed. Lindy, however, still seemed distant, and after a while he felt a little surge of resentment. It didn't bother him, so why should it bother her? He had seen the reaction before, of course. There are those, mostly very self-centered ones, who cannot stand the sight of a handicapped or mutilated body, identifying with it, imagining that it has happened to their own bodies. Usually he had no use for such people so why did it bother him so much with Lindy? Probably because he valued her for having been Frank's wife. Frank had known, and he obviously had not told Lindy. Because he just hadn't thought about it? Or because he knew her so well, knew her as one to whom an amputation stump is obscene, who feels that an amputee should not embarrass real people by appearing in public.

He decided that he really didn't give a damn, but there was a pall on the evening nevertheless. There was some more shoptalk, then an exchange of war tales between the men, a lot of woman talk. The two children were allowed—a bet is a bet—to stay up until nine o'clock.

When Lindy and Leigh went to put them to bed, each of the girls having kissed everyone good-night at least twice just to delay the ordeal of bedtime, Tusk reminded Warren that he'd like a chance to meet Angelo Bardoni in a work situation.

"No sweat," Bob said. "I'll make a call before I leave for work in the morning."

"And this Bardoni fought Frank to a bloody draw?" Tusk asked.

"I guess you could call it that."

"Nothing personal, just work differences?"

"As far as I know. I could have almost predicted a fight; it was just a matter of who Frank was going to hit. It was getting so tense that he had to hit someone or something."

"He ever have a fight before?"

"No. He was big enough that most of the time no one bucked him too much, but Bardoni is big, too. And he's a smart-ass. He doesn't like to take orders. With the hairy-chest type you just

have to demonstrate now and then who's top
dog.''

A man had to be pretty good to fight Frank to a
draw, unless Frank had really let himself get out
of condition. They both had done a little boxing
in the Golden Gloves, and in the service. Frank
was tough and fast. Tusk found himself looking
forward to meeting Bardoni, and knew, with a
little nagging hint of near shame, that he felt his
manhood challenged by proxy, because Frank,
who could always hold his own with him, had
been held to a draw.

Lindy called it a night at ten. Tusk kissed Leigh
on the cheek, shook Bob's hand, went out and
started to open the door of the van for Lindy. She
beat him to it and climbed in. She was silent,
speaking only when she had to remind him of the
route home. He said that the Warrens were nice
people, ventured an opinion that the weather
suited him, hot in the day, cool in the evenings.
He pulled the van into the driveway and started
to get out to open the door for her, and she once
again beat him to it. Doggedly he walked around
the front of the van anyhow. She slammed the
door and looked directly at him for the first time
since early that evening.

''I want you to come inside,'' she said.

''It's late.''

''Please,'' she said.

Inside, she walked through the living room to
the kitchen, poured drinks, left him standing in

the archway to the dining room to watch her economy of movement, her grace as she quickly did the chore. When she turned, her face was serious. She had the drinks in her hand, put them down on the cabinet, folded her arms over her breasts.

"I'm sorry," she said.

"For what? It was a nice evening."

"I was shocked. I didn't know. You seem so—"

"So whole?" he asked. He laughed. "It even has its advantages sometimes. I can use them to crack nuts or drive a nail."

"You did that for my benefit, didn't you?" she asked, still very serious. "The race, I mean."

He in his turn was shocked. He was long past the need to show off his muscles for girls. But she'd nailed him. He was a man who knew what he was doing, and there were times when he did things that, if given a choice, he would have chosen not to do, but they were things that needed doing and until recently he'd had no plans not to go on doing them.

"You've never been married," she said.

"No," he answered, but his mind was racing. When had it started to go wrong? In North Carolina when he miscalculated for the first time and had to have his chestnuts pulled out of the fire by another operative? In Arizona where he'd put himself into a position of exposure and had to call, once again for help?

"When did it happen?" she asked.

He had to jerk himself back into the present. "During the search-and-destroy phase," he said.

"Frank told me how you got your name. That general, your friend. He said the American army was like a tuskless elephant, threshing around in the bush. You were to be the tusk, a sharp weapon to probe and kill."

"And I pushed where I should have probed," he said. This time there would be no call for aid. This time it was personal. This time he'd do the job himself. And this business of trying to regain his lost youth, of showing off for the wife of an old friend. Hell, she was all girl, but she was Frank's wife. But didn't the light from the fluorescent fixture make her hair gleam like molten silver?

"What happened?" she asked.

"A land mine. I was lucky. I fell backward just as it went off."

"Lucky," she echoed in a whisper.

"Do I get that drink or are you saving it for an emergency?" he asked, not liking his thoughts.

"Not yet," she said. There was a slight sway to her hips as she walked to him, five, six steps, the length of the kitchen vinyl, her eyes on his, arms coming up before she reached him, standing on tiptoe as he was frozen, her lips, large and soft, parting to press gently, sweetly, on his. So soft, once, twice, three times, pecking on, and to the side, and below his lips, and there was a feeling in him that startled him, a breathless trembling feeling that he hadn't known since he hunted girls with old Frank and, finding a nice one, knew that youthful and somehow beautifully innocent lust. He felt his arms lift, find the indentation of waist, so delightfully female, the smell of her in his nose, clean hair and soap from the shower after the swim. He found her lips and there was no more softness, no pecking, but an ignition of fire, a sudden knowledge that one of nature's minor miracles had exploded.

There are girls and there are girls. He was not without his knowledge of girls. But only once before had there been the miracle, the knowing, the realization that all is right and that every cell, every fiber of two human beings, is attuned, calling out to each other. He drank of her, knowing the softness of lip, the sweetness of inner mouth. And then he pushed her roughly away.

She had a little smile on those soft lips, lifted her hand to touch them gently with the back of her hand.

"Lady," he said, "it is time for me to get the hell out of here."

"Now do you believe that it's all right, that I am truly sorry?" she asked.

"Lindy, my feet, or lack of them, are not what's bothering me right now."

"I know," she said, drawing a step closer.

"You're Frank's wife," he said.

"And you're his best, lifelong friend."

"And Brutus was an honorable man," he said, trying for a grin, not making it.

She pressed to him. He kept his hands at his side. "That doesn't happen too often."

"No," he said, for that sudden closeness made him feel as if he knew her every thought.

"I'm alone," she said. "I'm wept out and lonely and alone and that's only happened to me once before in my life, and that makes me one of the lucky ones." She was whispering, her face turned up, her lips moving, showing that miracle, that movement, that invitation.

At the last moment, entering Frank's bedroom, he came near bolting, running for it; but ahead of him there was a trail of feminine garments and on the bed there was—

Lindy.

Lindy. She was clean and smooth, young and healthy and elastic and warm. Later she spoke to him, lying on her back in darkness, in the quiet of early morning.

"What do I call you?"

"Just so you call," he said.

"Not Tusk. That's hard and impersonal."

"My given name is G.W.," he said. "As on thousands of army forms, G-no-given-name, W-no-middle-name, Smith."

"Frank always called you G.W.," she said. "And usually the full name, G.W. Smith."

Old Frank. Dead. Flesh kept from rotting by chemicals pumped into his empty veins, lying there under the ground and drying up slowly, slowly, inside a couple of thousand bucks' worth of bronze and satin lining. Frank's bed. Frank's wife.

It had started to go wrong in North Carolina, where it was a simple and open case of greed and murder, and there'd been a woman, one of the lost ones, naked in a kudzu patch in the heart of Atlanta, and no kisses, just cruelty and fear as he forced her to talk about a murder. And another woman in Arizona, no kisses, no love, for she was protecting another murderer, and Tusk had come damned close to being killed by her. And it had led to this. To Frank's bed. To Frank's wife.

"Darling?" she whispered, turning to put her head on his shoulder.

"That pretty little widow have anything to do with your staying?" Anna Larch had asked.

God damn, was that it?

No. No, God damn it. He'd stayed because Frank had been killed and there wasn't anyone to see that there was justice. Maybe this would be the last one. Maybe when this one was over he'd finish. There were others to do the job. Hell, even a woman could do it. Zed had pulled him out of trouble twice. He was getting too old for it. Old and tired, thirty-five going on a hundred, and maybe he didn't have the stomach for it anymore. Frank's death had hit him hard. He'd lost friends before, but not like Frank. And death stank. Death was bodies of men blasted by auto-

matic weapons and mortars and grenades; death
was the quick leap, the closing of the piano-wire
noose around a neck, the quick leap back to
escape the spouting blood. Death was Frank
screaming as he fell five hundred feet to smash
himself obscenely onto concrete, and maybe he'd
had enough.

There'd always be the case where the law-
enforcement people were helpless, the case
where fat, comfortable judges who'd never been
victims of violence forgot that the right to life is
man's most basic freedom, that the taking of life
is still the most serious of all brutalities and must
be punished accordingly. There'd always be
those cases, and not even the organization could
mete out eye-for-an-eye justice in all of them,
and after this one they'd just have to find someone else. The old boat was still back there in the
marina on the North Carolina coast, and thanks
to his partners and the land development he
would have enough money to spend the rest of
his life puttering around up and down the coast-
line, taking her down to the Keys in the winter
and into the splendid waterways of the mid-
Atlantic coast in the summer. Water birds following, looking for bits of food tossed over; fish
waiting to be eaten; sun, water, peace.

Alone? Well, he was basically a loner. Had
always been. Frank Pitt was the only human being who had ever been privy to his innermost
thoughts. He'd had friends and friends, but

Frank was the only, to use a feminine term, soul mate he'd ever known. And here he was in Frank's bed, wondering if Frank's wife liked boats and water and sun.

"Darling, what is it?" she asked, and he thought, wryly, that she'd solved the problem of what to call him. "Were you thinking about Frank?"

"Off and on," he said.

"I'll never stop thinking of him. I don't think you'd want me to." She raised herself on one elbow. He could see her face, framed by loosely hanging hair, in the glow of moonlight coming through the open window. "I was remembering how he used to talk about the things you two did when you were in high school. I remember that he used to laugh when he talked about the fight you two had over the little blonde. He said that he and G.W. Smith had always had the same taste in girls."

It was bitter inside him.

"Darling, let me say this. I think if Frank could look back and see us, if he could send us a message from some cloud somewhere, that he'd say, 'Hey, kids, good for you.'"

"Yeah," he said. "I guess we can tell ourselves that."

"But you're feeling guilty that you've betrayed your friend."

"Lindy, I guess I just need a little time to think."

"All right. Me, too. I told myself when he was killed that I loved him so much I'd never want another man. And it's been so short a time and—"

He put his arm around her. "We can also tell ourselves that it wasn't our fault, that it was fate, chemistry."

"You're a cynical son of a bitch, aren't you?" she asked, trying to draw away.

"I'll admit to a heavy and perhaps juvenile case of the guilts," he said. "And from what you just said, I'm not alone."

"No, damn you," she said. He let her pull away, got out of bed, got into his feet and his clothing.

She came into his arms as he was leaving the room, nude, warm, moist. "We can also say that I'm just a weak woman," she said. "That I need a man, a strong man like Frank."

"We'll give it some time, Lindy."

"Fair enough."

In his arms she was all he'd ever wanted. He could not bring himself to go. He talked. "Lindy, I can't say that I've never been in love."

"Who was she?"

"She was Vietnamese," he said. "Half-French."

"Was she very beautiful?"

"I thought so. Very."

"What happened?"

"A bomb. I had my land mine, she had her

bomb in a bicycle basket, left parked outside her father's store in Saigon. She was coming out to meet me when it went off.''

"Oh, God.'' Her soft lips were doing that wondrous thing, moving lightly around his mouth. "Oh, darling.''

"Maybe someday, when this is over, we can solve the problem, Lindy. Right now I'm a little confused. You hit me like a ton of bricks, lady. I need some air and some time and I need to find out who killed Frank and then—''

He hadn't meant to say that.

"Who k-k-illed him? Do you mean—''

Well, the damage, if any, was done. He'd meant to spare her that, let her go on thinking that it was an accident. She had already accepted that, a cruel fate, a senseless accident. Now she'd have to readjust, think of someone pushing Frank down that long fall.

But the damage was done. Another sign that he was losing it, that it was time to quit.

"Someone pushed him,'' he said.

"Oh, God, no,'' she moaned. "Oh, no.''

8

A BIG COFFEE URN was set up on level four, in a
space along one wall. The level was packed with
conduits and piping, a part of the cooling system
that reclaimed the steam after it had given of its
superheated pressurized power to the turbines.
Angelo Bardoni's pipe-fitting crew was at work
removing bad welds—some of the very ones that
Frank Pitt had black-lined in his last inspection.
But Bardoni had not yet made an appearance.

There were four men in the crew, three of them
young, the other a man in his fifties perhaps, a
sun-wrinkled face, graying hair, a set of perfect
dentures that looked out of place in his weathered
face. Tusk had picked him to ask, on his arrival, if
there was anything he needed to do.

"Don't ask me," the older man said. "I ain't
the boss."

So he waited. He sampled the coffee, found it
to be freshly made, decent. He found a wooden
crate and sat. The old man, coffee cup in hand,
came over, leaned, said, "They don't like to see
you sitting."

"What difference does it make if there's no work to be done?" Tusk asked, but he slid off the crate and stood.

"Name's Dick," the older man said, extending the hand not holding the coffee cup.

"Smith," Tusk said. "When does everyone go to work?"

Dick shrugged. "Last time I saw a man work was in 1944, before the war ended."

"I sure don't see anything here for a carpenter," Tusk said.

"Where were you before?" Dick asked.

"Working for a private contractor in North Carolina," Tusk said.

"Union?"

"Nope."

"Had to drive a nail or two, huh?"

"One or two."

"I started out in the mines," Dick said. "My dad got me a job when I was sixteen. He was a dedicated union man, and he had a reason to be. They used to kill a lot of men in them mines where spending a dollar or two would have saved 'em. I did my share of walking the lines. Threw a few rocks. Talk about proud, when I got my journeyman's card my feet didn't touch the ground, and by God I earned it!"

Neither had noticed the approach of a new man. "Why don't you stop talking, old man?" Angelo Bardoni asked.

"It's a free country," Dick said.

"Who the hell are you?" Bardoni demanded, glaring at Tusk. He was about six-two, coal-black beard stubble adding to the swarthiness of his face, chest and arms showing muscles that could have been developed by pumping iron.

"Carpenter," Smith said.

"Where's the regular man?" Bardoni asked.

"All I know is they told me to report to Bardoni. I guess that's you."

Dick was walking away. "Pop," Bardoni said, "there's a weld ready; get your ass in gear."

"Don't need you to tell me when to go to work," Dick said over his shoulder.

The expression that came over Bardoni's face made him look like a man capable of murder, but then a lot of people who wouldn't ever commit an act of violence looked capable of it, while those who did kill often looked surprisingly innocent.

"When you have something for me to do, just tell me," Tusk said.

"Here's what you can do. You can get your ass down to the shack and tell them to send me my regular man."

"I don't think I'll do that," Tusk said. He put his coffee cup down onto the crate, stood as if relaxed, but his casual attitude was deceptive. He was balanced, ready to move fast.

"Listen, Jo-Jo, I'm the boss here," Bardoni said, moving closer to thrust his face near Tusk's.

"My union says different," Tusk said. "As the

only carpenter on the job, I'm my own boss. I
work with you, not for you."

For a moment he thought it was going to begin,
but after a few seconds of menacing glaring Bardoni turned, went to the coffee urn, slapped it
viciously with his palm before drawing a cup. He
came back to face Tusk.

"All right," he said. "Get your ass to work.
This place needs cleaning up. You'll find a broom
over there."

"Negative on that, friend," Tusk said.

"You disobeying my orders?"

"You know better than to tell a journeyman
carpenter to sweep up," Tusk said, ready, almost
wanting it, thinking of Frank taking punishment
from the big dark-faced man. But Bardoni didn't
throw a punch. Instead he lifted his foot quickly,
stomped it down on the toe of Tusk's work shoes.
He shifted all his weight to it, grinning at Tusk.
Tusk stood calmly. The feet could take a lot more
punishment than that. Bardoni took his foot off,
still grinning.

"Least you wear good safety shoes," he said.
"Just testing."

"They're pretty good," Tusk said. He lashed
out, not hard enough to break a shinbone, but
hard enough, the weight of the artificial foot carrying itself, to crack painfully, to send someone
hopping around, cursing, bending to rub his shin.
If you give a man enough provocation, you can
learn, quickly, if he's capable of murder.

His eyes red, a film of tears forming from the pain, Bardoni stopped hopping and rubbing, stood and looked around, seized a length of three-inch pipe about five feet long. He crouched, began to advance slowly on Tusk. Dick jumped to seize his arm.

"You don't wanna do that, Angelo," he said.

Bardoni threw the old man aside with one arm movement, sending him crashing against a set of pipes to fall to the floor.

"You're damned mean with an old man," Tusk said.

"You son of a bitch," Bardoni said, still advancing. Tusk was picking out a place to go.

"But with a man your own size you need help, huh, big fellow?" Tusk asked.

Bardoni stopped, straightened up. He looked down at the pipe in his hand and then tossed it, clanging, to one side. He came in one rush, big arms extended. Tusk sidestepped and tapped him, not too hard, on the nose. It was enough to start blood, and the big man turned, rubbed his nose, looked at the blood on his hand.

"Fight," someone yelled.

He was more careful, fists up this time, coming in pushing one foot forward. He was carrying his guard too low, however, and it was easy to dance in, tap him on the nose again, starting the blood flowing more freely.

"Anytime you want to quit, big man," Tusk taunted.

Bardoni roared, a sound of pure rage, pushed in, arms and fists flailing. He could hit, the blows hurting Tusk's arms as he blocked them, but he was no boxer, just a brawler; and the outcome was inevitable. He got in one good blow that sent the white dots dancing in front of Tusk's eyes and gave him an appreciation for the man's strength, and then Tusk went to work methodically, looking not too graceful, but dancing, weaving, moving, fists lashing out. He didn't want to end it too quickly, was taking a decided pleasure in it, remembering Frank. He had to put Bardoni down three times before he stayed, looking up in dazed wonder.

"God damn," Bardoni muttered, wiping blood. "You have to cut me up?"

"You're a hard man to stop, Angelo," Tusk said.

"Could have told me you're a goddamned ring boxer," Bardoni said, shaking his head and pushing himself up. "I ain't no goddamned fool."

"I'll tell you next time."

"Man," Bardoni said, "there ain't gonna be no next time. If there is, I won't throw away the pipe." He held out his hand. "Fair and square."

"Fair and square," Tusk said.

And that was that. In anger, yes. But Frank hadn't been killed in a swift burst of anger. He'd been lured to the place of his death, a calculated thing, not Bardoni's style.

"Sorry," Tusk said, still shaking hands with the pipe fitter. "You pushed me pretty hard."

"Wanna know what a man's made of when he works for me," Bardoni said. "You're one of them sons of bitches got razor blades on their knuckles."

"You wouldn't be bad if you'd learn to keep your right up," Tusk said.

Bardoni dropped his hand. "I'm too old to take lessons. How 'bout some coffee, champ?"

"My pleasure," Tusk said, stepping over to fill two cups.

"Lots of sugar," Bardoni said. He turned. "All right, you bastards, let's get a little bit of work done."

Later Tusk made it a point to be alone with Dick, the old man. He was beginning to get a case of the guilts again, first showing off for a girl and then provoking a fight so he could take revenge for a dead man.

"Angelo's gonna develop an inferiority complex," Dick said quietly, so as not to be heard. "That's two in a row he's been cut up."

"Yeah?" The old man wanted to talk. Questions would be unnecessary.

"Young start-up engineer, 'bout two, three months back. Fought head to head for a half hour. Both of them just about out on their feet."

"Angelo doesn't get along with start-up?"

"He don't get along with many," Dick said. "Kept pushing this Frank Pitt. Fellow fell down the bay."

"I heard," Tusk said.

"Kept pushing and then this Pitt finally said, 'Okay, Angelo, if that's the only way.' We all went down and outside. They had blood and sand all over."

"Any hard feelings afterward?"

"Naw. Anything Angelo respects, it's a fellow tough as he is or tougher. Heard him tell one of the men that even if Pitt was a bastard he wasn't all bad, at that."

By quitting time Tusk had not lifted a hammer or a saw. The crew had done a couple of welds, sparks showering. He'd drunk a half dozen cups of coffee with Bardoni, who liked to talk and tell about brawls he'd won in bars and on the job.

It was only the fact that his judgment had been so bad of late that kept Tusk from taking Angelo Bardoni off the list entirely. But he'd been wrong too much in the past couple of years. He wasn't writing anyone off, not just yet. He declined, with an excuse that he was meeting someone after work, Angelo's invitation to stop off for a couple of brews on the way into town, went to the construction shack to punch out on the time clock, smiled as he did so. He'd be paid for eight hours' work at a pretty fair wage. He hadn't hit a lick.

She was waiting for him near the gate to the parking lot, dressed in her blue guard's uniform, slacks seeming to be tailor-made, blouse and tunic hiding her breasts. Her light hair was bunned under the visor cap.

He hadn't realized how beautiful the day was until he saw her, saw the smile begin on her face, felt a surge inside, remembering the softness, the sweetness of her.

"Hi, lady," he said. "If you're waiting around the gate to pick up a construction worker—"

"Sounds like a good idea," she said.

"One volunteer," he said. "I'll even buy you a drink in the working man's bar."

"I'm on duty," she said. "I thought you might like to take a ride."

"Sure, where?" Forgotten, the good intentions of the past night; forgotten, the guilt, the resolve to stay away until he could find Frank's killer, until he could get his head straightened out.

"I've got to make a tour of the reservation. No reason why we can't make it a sight-seeing tour for you."

The vehicle was a Toyota jeep, son of a Land Rover, as the TV ads said, brawny, rough riding, open. She drove it with a flair, sand and pebbles flying, sun causing her to squint. He was looking at her face, in profile, as they drove away from the plant out into the sagebrush flats, past a fenced-off area with signs that warned of radiation.

"You're supposed to be looking at the scenery," she said, turning to flash him a smile. "But if I read what I think I read in your eyes—"

"The sand would be too hot," he said.

"That's a low-level dump we just passed," she said.

"Radioactive waste?"

"Yep. They're here and there out here in the desert."

"Does it make you feel a little shaky inside and want to breathe deeper?" he asked.

"I think that's my aura you're feeling," she said. "At the moment it's putting out all sorts of radiation, the little devil."

A sandy rut arrowed straight out from the plant, down far and away toward the river. She kept the speedometer at about thirty-five, and there were times when he had to hang on. The government reactors came into view. Steam or smoke was coming from the tall stacks of only one.

"What's to keep someone from just wandering in here?" he asked.

"Fences along the highways. It would be simple, though. I don't see why anyone would want to come in. But there's always the possibility. That's why we patrol at irregular intervals."

"Any danger of getting a dose of radiation out here?"

The jeep bounced over a partially covered and rusted rail line. "You'd have to be determined to get it," she said. "Do a lot of digging. It's all buried real deep. They make regular tests out here. None of it escapes into the air. It's all under the sand." She pointed. "There's one of the old bunkers. The mean ones."

"What's in there?"

"Big stuff. Old reactor-core parts. They loaded them on flatcars and pulled the cars on rails right into the bunkers, then covered them over, deep. Needless to say, they pulled the flatcars with the stuff on them from a distance."

"That's one of the biggest problems of all, isn't it?" he asked.

"One that hasn't been solved yet. The Sweetwater site is one of the chief dumping grounds for the whole industry. Radioactive waste comes here from all over the country. When they start pumping the contaminated water out of Three Mile, it'll probably be brought here and buried, unless the environmentalists raise too much hell about it. The governor closed it down here a while back, and the stuff began to pile up all over the country."

She had turned, was driving parallel to the river, the government reactors bigger than life now, up close.

"Just one working?" Tusk asked.

"At the moment. That and the fast-flux reactor, the breeder reactor. Most of them are obsolete. It happens fast in this business. They'll have to find a place to store the hot stuff from the old graphite-core reactors someday."

"No power lines," Tusk said.

"No. The government reactors are used in weapons production and research. The fast-flux plant could generate a lot of electricity, but since

it's experimental it'll be taken up and down a
lot." She pointed again. "There's another of the
big dumps. Used-up core elements on flatcars inside." The mound of earth rose high, spread out
in a rough oval, already overgrown with sagebrush.

"Can you go in those things?"

"You could. There's an entrance. A couple of
right-angle radiation traps. Now and then someone opens the door and thrusts in an instrument
to see if the stuff is leaking around the radiation
traps."

"Too hot to go inside?"

"You take one step around the last right-angle
radiation trap, then one more step before you're
dead. It measures in the hundreds of rems in
there. In a few thousand years they'll have to
begin to worry about what to do with it."

"And meanwhile there are more cores being
used up."

"And by-products and medical waste and contaminated material."

They were now moving back toward the plant.
A prairie hawk soared over them, examining
them from a height low enough that they could
see its head swiveling alertly. And he knew that
he would go to her again, that night, when she
got home from work.

"I think the problem can be solved," she said,
not noticing his change of mood. "The way it's
stored here works and can work for a long time.

In the long run we might be able to, oh, use the space shuttle to shoot the wastes out into space."

"Into the sun?"

"Maybe, but I don't know about that. The sun is, of course, just a huge atomic reactor gone wild, but we don't know what effect dumping a rocketload of waste onto the surface would have. What if we stimulated a sunspot or something? A storm on the sun puts out more radioactive particles than we've released on earth since the first bomb. I think just send it into an escape orbit, send it flying forever and away."

"Give some little green spaceman a nasty surprise."

"Any little green man with the technology to be out there in space would have enough sense to monitor it before he opened it up."

"You're pro-nuke all the way," Tusk said.

"It's catching. You live with a man who believes in it and you begin to believe, in spite of the problems. Frank didn't want his children and his grandchildren to have to face a steadily decreasing standard of living. He felt that the plants could be built to operate safely. He said sloppy work and ignorance, not the nuclear reactors, were the enemies."

"You wanted children, you and Frank?" he asked.

"Yes. We kept putting it off." She looked at him, eyes squinted, a hint of a line of weariness around her splendid mouth. "I wanted children more than Frank, I suppose. The time just never seemed to be right."

Children. The Smith family, all of them that he knew, had been towheads when young, cotton-haired little boys and girls. And Lindy was a flaxen blonde. Their children would come out fair haired. A little girl looking like Lindy.

"What time will you be over?" she asked as she parked the jeep near the guard station.

No question about it. "You name it."

"I can leave early. Ten? Give me time to have a shower."

"Nine," he said. "After being in the desert you need your back scrubbed."

"Gee," she said, her smile soft, suggestive. "I didn't know you were intelligent and considerate as well as almost handsome."

The smile was contagious. "What the hell you mean, almost?" he asked. She was leaning toward him, as if drawn, as if unable to stop herself. She jerked back with a sigh.

9

THE HONEY-SKINNED WOMAN lay on a large towel on freshly mowed grass away from the hotel swimming pool. She wore the briefest bikini, not for enticement, but to allow the burning August sun to touch as much as possible. There was no breeze. Sweat formed on her stomach and pooled in the indentation of her navel. Her tawny hair was wet, curling more tightly to her finely shaped skull. Her eyes were closed behind the large dark sunshades, but she was not asleep.

This time she had chosen a different hotel; Jamaica's North Shore was becoming too crowded, too peopled by salesmen on vacation. She did not come for company. She drank little, ate when she was hungry, spent as many as eight hours a day in the sun, baking, sweating, dozing and letting her mind idle. In a way it was a form of punishment, the breathless heat, the sodden feel of the sweat-soaked bikini, skin drying to be moistened by applications of Bain de Soleil. But it worked.

In the afternoon she climbed down the cliff

face to the sea, clear azure water showing, from
the top of the cliff, darker coral formations.
From the top of the cliff she could see Port An-
tonio. Across the narrow stretch of sea below,
the tropical beauty of San-San, Princess Island,
heavily palmed, picture-postcard wonder, a bit
of the South seas. Water warm to her sun-heated
body, the stretching out of muscles, swimming
out in the channel, past the island, alone in the
sea, no boats, no swimmers, long powerful
strokes carrying her out and out until there was
only the challenge of getting back to fall in total
exhaustion onto the sand. Another form of punishment, but it toned the long feminine muscles,
held the shape of a body that got its share of ad-
miring looks.

She rarely went to the dining room, and when
she did she ignored the inviting smiles. She spoke
only when giving an order, tipped generously,
making up to the staff for her lack of friend-
liness.

Every other day she spoke into the telephone.

"How is the weather, Oscar?"

The answer varied, Oscar's Bostonian accent
coming down the long distance with that curious
ring, proper and informal at the same time. After
ten days in Jamaica she had yet to hear, in
Oscar's friendly comments on the weather, the
word that would put her aboard the small plane
for the trip to Kingston and a jetliner headed
north and west.

Meanwhile there was the sun and the sea to test her, and the forgetfulness of falling exhausted into her bed to sleep until the sun woke her with its first rays.

10

IT RARELY RAINS on the high desert in August. The sprinklers run in the evenings, dampening the perfect lawns around the newly constructed houses of the developments, and in the agricultural areas of the basin that, said either Mr. Lewis or Mr. Clark, would never be capable of supporting life, the nectarines ripen. The desert shows areas of green fruit trees, pole beans climbing ten feet high, and the production is limited only by the amount of water available from the streams. In bad years the smaller streams that drain into the mighty river are low, and there is the threat of a water cutoff, allotments used up, while the fruit is still on the trees.

It is an area of contrast. A ride west from town in a Volkswagen camper, cold beer on ice, a long-legged blond girl in shorts at one's side, can show extreme contrasts within a few hours' drive, from the barren, sun-baked brown deadness of the hills to the rich green groves of the valley to the sudden release from desert heat in the foothills. And then the snow-domed mountain and crisp cool nights with the camper windows open, the lovely feel of girl under a blanket.

They left on a Friday afternoon, set up camp in the coolness of a mountain night, swam in bracingly chill mountain water, a weekend of love and not thinking, except of each other.

It was enough to give a man the guilts, and he was suffering them on Monday when he picked up Bob Warren for the drive to the site. Ten days. What the hell was he doing? Punching a time clock, earning pretty good money that he didn't need, learning nothing more than what he'd learned in the first few days. He wasn't in the mood to talk, and Bob Warren seemed to sense it.

After a couple of days with Bardoni's crew, he'd been reassigned, was scheduled to work outside the plant. What had seemed to be a good idea was going sour. He did not have the mobility he needed, the access he needed. His thoughts went too often to Lindy. He had begun to lose his effectiveness in North Carolina, and on this one he was next to useless. All he'd accomplished to date was to convince himself, with only his own judgment of character to back it up, that Angelo Bardoni had not pushed Frank off the top. It was necessary to make something happen. The only problem was, he didn't know what.

However, luck plays a part in every aspect of human life, and at midmorning, as he worked in the sun, taking some satisfaction in doing a good job of toenailing studs for some sort of temporary wooden building, luck played for him. He was told that he was wanted in start-up, to report to Bob Warren. He mopped his face with his handkerchief and put away his tools, stashed them in the locker and made his way to Warren's office.

Bob Warren was not there. Instead, the young graduate engineer, Mark Lingate, looked up from his desk. "Bob will be back shortly," he said. "He's at a hearing on the little wobble the other day."

"What's up?" Tusk asked.

"He's got something wrong with his chair and wants you to fix it."

Tusk sat down at Warren's desk. The air conditioning was cooling his sweat-soaked shirt, causing a little chill on his shoulders.

"I want to talk to you before Bob gets back," Mark Lingate said.

"Sure."

"There's something going on around here," Lingate said, looking very young and very serious.

Tusk raised his eyebrows to show interest.

"There are those who don't think Frank Pitt fell by accident," Lingate said. "I'll admit that I wasn't, at first, one of them."

For the first time in days he was alert, ready. "What changed your mind?"

"This," Lingate said, taking a piece of brown paper bag from his pocket.

It was folded roughly. Tusk opened it. The first

thing that caught his eye was a crude drawing of a skull and bones in a little pile, drops running out of them. The lettering said, REMEMBER WHAT HAPPENED TO ANOTHER SMART-ASS.

Bob Warren chose that time to come banging into the cubicle, his face dark. Tusk folded the paper and handed it back.

"It's all right," Mark said. "I showed it to Bob."

The question in Tusk's mind was why he'd been shown the piece of paper. He would have liked to get his hands on it, compare the printing with that which was on another piece of brown paper bag, the one he'd found among Frank's papers, but he was reasonably sure that it was the same.

"Looks as if you've made someone mad," he observed, rising. "Understand you want me to do some work," he said to Bob, making it clear that he wasn't too interested in Lingate's problem.

"Yeah," Bob said. "You ready?"

Ernest Martin walked into the office, smiling. "Bob, Bob," he said, "you knew it would mean a fine."

"Damn it, Martin, this plant is years behind schedule."

"But must you always blame it on me and my poor little union?" Martin asked, smiling and spreading his hands.

Warren grunted.

"I've met you somewhere," Martin said to Tusk.

No use playing coy. A man didn't get into a position like Martin's by not remembering faces. "At Belinda Pitt's house," he said.

"Ah, yes. And how is Mrs. Pitt holding up?"

"As well as can be expected," he said.

"You're working with us?"

"That's right," Tusk said.

"Well, you're keeping bad company, good union man like you." He smiled at Bob to show he wasn't really serious.

Tusk shrugged. Suddenly it seemed that everyone knew a lot about him. Martin made a parting remark and pranced—it could only be described as such—away.

"Well," Tusk said, "he wears nice suits."

"Bastard's probably putting the arm on every contractor who hires a pipe fitter," Bob growled.

That was the kind of thing he was supposed to think of, Tusk told himself. He made a mental note to get Frank's papers out, to go over them again carefully. The French say, look for the woman. G.W. Smith said, look for the man who stands to make a profit. And there had been that note, late in the sequence of Frank's papers, about Martin.

"Can you make me a list of contractors who use pipe fitters?"

"I guess so."

It was nearly lunchtime.

"I can dig most of them out of my files," Bob said. "You bring a lunch?" Tusk nodded. "Get it and come and we'll chew in the office while I plow through.''

The assignment man in the construction shack asked him casually if he was going to honor the company by doing any work that day, and Tusk said that he hadn't finished with carpentry stuff in the office yet. He was not at all content with himself. It was time to push. It was time to stop dreaming about a woman and get to it. Having Bob Warren gather information for him had its advantages and its disadvantages. One of the disadvantages sat at his desk, pouring iced tea from a thermos and eating sandwiches as Bob began to look through papers in manila folders on his desk. Mark, after trying a couple of times to start a conversation, was silent. Tusk copied information from letterheads into a small notebook.

''You guys just aren't going to tell me what's going on, huh?'' Lingate asked, after a long silence filled only with the crackling of paper and the clicking of Tusk's jaw as he chewed. Once a tough Cuban marine had landed a good one, almost ending it in the first round, and his jaw had popped ever since.

''I'm just giving Smith the names of a few companies,'' Bob said. ''He doesn't like it here in paradise.''

''Thought I might try over around Seattle,'' Tusk said.

''You guys know each other before?'' Mark asked.

"No," Bob said. "But I figure any man who can take Bardoni deserves a little help."

"Yeah," Mark laughed. "I sure wouldn't want to try."

Tusk had a list of a dozen contractors. "That's enough," he said. "If that doesn't do it I can always draw unemployment."

Bob looked at his watch. "Well, time to make a dollar."

Lingate showed no signs of hurry. "How's it going with you, Mark?" Bob asked. "Need any help?"

"Thanks, but things are pretty smooth."

"They won't be if you spend the day in the office," Bob said.

"I appreciate your concern," Lingate said coldly, "but I'm doing the job, Warren."

"Sure," Bob said. Tusk followed him out. "He took over Frank's section. He's not ready. They're trying to bring someone in to take over. He's gonna be one mad young college grad when he finds out."

It was difficult, but he was thinking again, reviewing, planning ahead. Something tugged at his mind. "Someone told me that there were two engineers with degrees working under Frank."

"Yeah, Mark and Stuart Bennett."

"I haven't seen Bennett around the office," Tusk said.

"Stuart's a loner," Bob said. "He has a knack of staying out of the way."

"Did he and Frank get along?"

"Yeah, I guess so. You can't really tell with Stuart. I fear he likes the bottle a little bit too much. He's a smart man, but unlike our Marky boy he has no ambition. He should be a union member; just wants to get along and draw his paycheck."

"No resentment about working under a man without a degree?"

"I don't know. Stuart doesn't talk much. I can probably dig him out of his hiding place if you'd like to meet him."

Tusk shrugged. It was like grasping at straws. He followed Bob's lope, joined him in an empty elevator.

"You didn't say anything about that little threat Mark got," Bob said.

"Does that happen often?"

"There's always some resentment against supervisors. I'd guess that Mark's pushing pretty hard, trying to hold onto the job he moved into by default. Probably just some fellow he chewed out. I don't think it means much."

Tusk started to tell him about a similar threat, decided against it.

They found Stuart Bennett on an upper level. For a change people seemed to be working. From several plastic-protected sites welding torches gleamed, and a crew was busy hoisting some mysterious piece of complicated-looking equipment into place with a small crane. Bob led the way through the usual maze of piping.

Bennett looked on first glance to be in his fifties. A closer look, however, showed the characteristic signs of the heavy drinker, the nose, the watery eyes. He was in a side room, empty of workers, still lingering over his lunch.

"How's it going, Stuart?" Bob asked. Bennett shrugged. "Well, thought I'd just check, see how you're getting along with young Lingate."

"Fine," Bennett said. "Least he's not afraid to climb up off the floor a few feet."

"Think he can handle the job?" Bob asked. Tusk was standing behind, acting the dutiful worker, waiting for the supervisor to take him along to his assigned task.

"Hell," Bennett said. "I don't know what they're teaching kids in school these days. It isn't engineering."

"Don't say anything, but you'll probably be getting a new man," Bob said.

"I've been meaning to talk to you about that," Bennett said. "Lingate's all right. When he gets a little experience he'll be a good man. And Pitt was a good man. Wasn't his fault he got dizzy climbing a ladder to inspect a job. I didn't say anything when they put him in the job. I guess he'd earned it. But there comes a time when a man has to speak. I'm no jerk myself. You know it, Warren. You know I can do a job. If you could find a way to put in a word for me I'd damned sure appreciate it."

"Well, Stuart, they don't listen to me too much on matters like that," Bob said, obviously uncomfortable.

"Maybe a letter, then," Bennett said. "I'm putting in a bid for the job. A letter from you might help. You do your job without causing too many waves. I think a letter from you would help."

"Sure, Stuart. Get on it tonight."

"I appreciate it."

"Does he want that job badly enough to kill for it?" Tusk asked as they walked away and down.

"The sad thing is," Bob said, "that he knows he hasn't got a chance at it. He cost a company about ten million dollars on his last job."

"How's that?"

"He was in charge of start-up when they started to roll the turbines on a plant up in Tennessee. He was drunk. Something went wrong and he panicked. He started overriding circuit breakers manually, burned up one hell of a lot of instrumentation."

"Jesus, I can see why Frank was worried about safety," Tusk said.

"He's in a position here where he can do no harm, and he knows his stuff. I'd take him in my section anytime. I'm surprised that he's even asking for Frank's job, though."

Another name added to the list. A drunk. A fallen man, a man who had held a good job and lost it and now wanted to start moving up again.

But it didn't figure. Frank could have handled a drunk, a man whose hands shook slightly as he talked. Tusk went back to the construction shack, told the dispatcher that he wasn't feeling well, left the plant. He had some thinking to do.

He did it in his room in Anna Larch's house, taking out Frank's notebooks and going over them a page at a time, serious now, working his way toward the end, more objective than he'd been the first time he read them. He'd learned just a short time before the first reading that Frank was dead. Now, devoid of emotionalism, he could read into the notes a hint of self-doubt, a hidden stridency. Much as he hated to admit it, it seemed that Frank had not had all the confidence he needed, had tried to buy it the cheap way by talking down others.

And yet there was a sincerity there. A man can have a character fault and still be a worthwhile human being. There was no doubt that Frank Pitt had been a dedicated man, a man who believed in giving honest work for an honest dollar, a man who took too much on himself in an almost idealistic desire to make the whole world run like a smoothly ticking watch. So Frank had taken on the world and lost.

And there, in the last pages, was the note: "*Get* Martin's ass *tomorrow*."

And on that *tomorrow*, he died.

There was a time in each case when he could almost anticipate the ending, could smell it, feel it. That he'd been wrong twice in the past two years gave him room for doubt, but things were beginning to add up. In that massive undertaking out there at the Sweetwater site billions of dollars were involved, thousands of men, more than a hundred individual contractors. When billions are being spent there is always opportunity for the greedy.

True, he had little to go on. What he had was a hunch, a feeling, but there had been times in the past when he could trust his feelings. And, fortunately, he had the means of exploring. He was thinking about the telephone when there was a little knock on his outside door.

Now how the hell, he thought, grinning, can you tell from a simple knock that the sound is being made by a set of feminine knuckles, attached to a graceful arm, attached to a shoulder clad in the blue of a guard's uniform leading to a face of smiling and radiant beauty?

"Since you're neglecting me I decided to pursue you," she said. She stepped in, closed the door behind her. So easy to become lost in a kiss.

When she broke the kiss he stepped back. "I was going to call later."

"No need to now. I've caught you." She pushed forward.

"I have a few things to do, Lindy. You run along like a good girl, and I'll be over in an hour or so."

"You're mean and hateful and if it's another woman I'll scratch her eyes out."

He laughed. "Possessive wench."

"You love it."

She was always saying things to surprise him, and the truth of the statement hit him, made him recognize something new about himself. He did. Her attachment to him, her desire to spend every moment possible with him, pleased him. He turned her, slapped her shapely behind playfully, opened the door. She stuck out her tongue.

"If it's more than an hour I'll come after you," she said.

Anna Larch was in her cluttered living room, trying to sew a patch on a pair of jeans. "Haven't seen much of you," she said when she opened the door.

"Making a dollar," Tusk said.

"Among other things." She let him in. "Coffee?"

He was thinking that if he hurried he might be able to get there in time to wash her back. "No, not this time, Anna. I'd like to use your telephone."

"You know where it is," she said, starting to sit down.

"Anna, I know it's rude as hell of me, but don't you need to walk down to the corner for a loaf of bread or something?"

"Ah," she said, "it's like that, is it?" She

smiled. "As a matter of fact, there's flowers in the backyard need watering."

"Thank you. You're a fine lady."

He gave his credit card number after dialing direct, heard Oscar's voice. "Ah, Tee. We've been expecting to hear from you."

"Need some help, Oscar." He didn't wait for acknowledgment. That's why Oscar was there. His was the only face ever seen in that establishment back in the East somewhere, a building that consisted, to Tusk's personal knowledge, of an entry hall, a room where Oscar presided, a cubicle with a walnut desk and one-way mirrors, and other unseen areas where wondrous things were accomplished.

"I want to know if any of the following companies are paying off a union official named Ernest Martin." He knew the conversation was being recorded. No need to talk slowly. He listed a dozen of the larger companies involved in hiring or working with pipe fitters at the site. "I want background on Ernest Martin." He paused for a moment.

"Yes, sir?" Oscar asked.

He didn't like to cost the company money. He had no idea how the establishment gathered some of the information he had reason to need from time to time, knew only that it had to be an extensive and expensive operation, reaching into unexpected places, from the files of the FBI, into the confidential files of huge corporations, down to the local level. He'd never gone into a city where there was not a friendly contact, if needed, on the metro police force. But he'd been wrong twice.

"I also want a background workup on a union worker named Angelo Bardoni, on an engineer named Stuart Bennett." Again he paused.

"Is that all, sir?"

"No," he said, taking a deep breath. "Give me the works on Robert B. Warren, on Mark Lingate." Pause. A feeling of hurt inside, an almost traitorous sinking of his stomach. "And, finally, on Mrs. Frank Pitt."

"I take it, sir, from the variety of your requests, that things are somewhat muddled."

"Right, Oscar. That's why I need it."

Oscar gave a polite little laugh. "Well, sir, after all, *someone* is paying for it."

He grinned wryly. Someone. Him. He hoped that his partners back in North Carolina were selling a lot of houses.

He went to the little fridge he'd bought in a secondhand store and brought out two frosty Dos Equis. He found Anna in the backyard watching the sprinklers work.

"Your reward, *madame*, for being so nice," he said.

"It wasn't a girl," she said, taking the bottle, "because the girl was just here."

He grinned. "You don't miss a trick."

"I don't spy," she said, smiling back at him. "I

just happen to want to know who's coming to my house, hoping vainly that it might be a visitor for me. Belinda looked quite well.''

"Yes," he said.

"And quite happy," Anna said, her eyes watching for his reaction. "Much happier than the last time I saw her."

"When was that?" Tusk asked.

"Before her husband was killed. I was visiting Mandy in their house."

"Anna, you're trying to tell me something," he said.

"I'm an old woman, Mr. Smith. It's really none of my business."

"Now come on, Anna. You don't hint and then back off."

She laughed. "No, I guess I didn't intend to. I guess I'm just a nosy old broad sticking my opinion in where it's not wanted."

"What was she unhappy about, Anna?"

"I've seen men in love, you know," she said with a little smile.

"Obvious, huh?"

"You look almost silly with that gloating little smile on your face all the time," she said. "But not really." She put a hand on his arm. "She's a lucky girl. I hope you're equally lucky."

"You're beginning to worry me," he said.

"Damnedest dumbest thing I've ever done," she said, looking away, "telling a man silly in love with a pretty girl things he doesn't want to hear. We talked about it, Mandy and I. But we're products of a different time. Things aren't what they used to be.''

"Anna," he said, feeling a void beginning to grow inside, "I think you're telling me that Lindy was—" Harsh words formed, did not come. "Ah, cheating on Frank?"

"Mind you, I didn't have the proof, but I saw the signs. The telephone calls at odd times— always when Frank was working. They were on a big push during that time. Working long hours. Now you think I'm just an old gossip."

"You must have your reasons," he said.

"Yes, damn it. I promised Mandy I wouldn't mention it, but—"

"Mandy?"

"I call her every so often. I've talked to her since you came here. I knew you weren't just a construction bum."

Jesus Christ, he was some successful investigator, with everyone in the state of Washington, seemingly, knowing that he was there for reasons other than what he wanted them to think.

"She wanted to tell you, and I said it might be better coming from a near stranger. Least you can get mad at me and tell me to butt out."

"The only way I'll be mad at you is if you let that good beer get hot." She drank and he mulled it over.

"Mandy said it was probably silly, but the way Frank was acting, something was wrong; and if it was trouble in the home nest she didn't want you being led astray by that.''

"You don't talk to many people, do you, Anna?'' he asked.

"Only when I get a chance, but don't worry. I have secrets that have been secrets since before you were born.''

"Thanks.''

"Hit you hard?''

"Yes and no, Anna. That was before I knew her. It hurts to think that she and Frank might have been nibbling away at each other, the way some people do when a marriage starts to go sour. Any idea about the other man?''

"Not a clue. She was out and around a lot. Active in wives' clubs, her job. *I'm* no detective, but the job would be the best place to meet a man, I'd think. She went to work because she said she didn't want to have to stay home by herself anymore, what with Frank working twelve hours a day and coming home beat. Then, when they put start-up back on eight hours, she had the job and it sometimes took her to work when he was home at night.''

"Want another beer?'' he asked.

"No. I guess you've got some thinking to do.''

He did. Funny, he'd never thought about her with Frank. After all, they'd been married. Frank had known her long before he met her. She was Frank's wife, and what had happened between them was all legal and normal; and

while he could, at times, wish that he had met
her first, maybe before Vietnam, there was not,
thinking of her with Frank, that little sickness in
the pit of his stomach that came as he thought
about what Anna had said. He considered calling
Mandy, but decided against it. Neither of the two
older women was stupid. If Anna said they had
no idea of the identity of the other man, then
Mandy could not help.

And, after all, it was merely suspicion, nothing
definite. They could be wrong. But, damn it,
women had a built-in radar for such things, could
tell you watching a woman at a party whether or
not she was ripe, already picked, or true-blue to
hubby.

They had, at times, talked about Frank. She
had asked him once if it bothered him for her
suddenly to remember things that had happened
with Frank and to mention them to him. He'd
said no, for it hadn't. Frank had been a part of
her life for years, and he would not think of trying to get her to forget, to destroy the good
memories. And she'd jokingly asked him about
the other women in his life.

"I want to know, and yet I don't want to
know," she'd said. "If I ask again, lie to me, darling."

So they'd talked, and she'd had every opportunity to confess, for on that long, lovely
weekend in the mountains there'd been mountains of talk, kid talk, "remember when" talk,

"do you like this" and "do you like that" talk, childhood memories shared, each trying to picture the other as a child, feeling somewhat deprived at having missed sharing childhood.

As he dressed he could remember the weekend clearly, could almost recreate the long, slow, whispered conversations in the van in the cool of the night. How she'd fallen in love a dozen times in high school and how she'd almost given in to a handsome psychology major, older than she, in her first year of college. Yes, she'd told him about things like that, explained, somewhat defensively, how she'd felt almost like a being from another world, holding on to old-fashioned ideas, taking her virginity to her marriage bed.

Logically, she could have lied to him, if only by omission, for people tend to forget things that go against their basic beliefs. Perhaps she was lying to herself as well as to him. If so, he could forgive. He could forgive her anything that had happened before she became a part of his life. There was no reason to hide anything from him, and although he had no morbid desire to hear sexual confessions from her, he would have been interested because the memories were a part of her; would have held her closely and told her that it was all right, that she'd never again have the need to seek out another man, that he would be her life, would be at her side always, for he was closer to her than he'd ever been to anyone.

He had expected her to be in her off-duty

uniform, form-fitting shorts. Instead, when she opened the door she was dressed prettily in a light summer frock. Her makeup was in place, so when he kissed her he was careful of the lipstick.

"I hate myself," she said. "I was looking forward to a long evening alone, just the two of us, and when Leigh called I said yes without thinking."

"Yes to what?"

"A bash. Leigh said it came up suddenly. Bob didn't want to watch television on a Saturday night, they called a few people, and it grew. Bob asked specifically that she call us, you."

In a way he was relieved. It would give him time to think about what Anna Larch had said. Looking at her, the light flowered, loosely flowing dress showing the sweetness of her body, he found it difficult to think of her in another man's arms. Betrayal of Frank got all mixed up in his mind with being betrayed himself, and he told himself that he was being an ass.

They were the first to arrive, so that Lindy could help Leigh with the snacks. He and Bob sat in the last rays of the evening sun and started to work on a jug of martinis.

The next to arrive was Mark Lingate. He came out of the house ahead of Leigh, she calling out, "Bob, Mark's here."

"Hey, hope I'm not busting in," Mark said. "I was just driving around and thought I'd come in and say hello."

"Glad you did, Mark," Bob said. "We're just boozing it up. Got a couple of people coming over. If I'd thought you'd be interested in sitting around with a bunch of old married folks I'd have called you."

"Well, I won't stay," Mark said. "I was just—"

"Hell, you're here, boy," Bob said. "Have a drink."

Lingate seemed ill at ease. Bob brought him a martini, waved him into a lawn chair. "Really, we're glad you dropped by. Stick around and see how the other half lives. We'll even waive the requirement that single men bring along a beautiful girl."

"Sure I won't be intruding?" Lingate asked.

"Hell, no."

"Well." He grinned. "I had a date, but she called it off at the last minute."

"Poor little boy," Bob said. "I pity your ass, young and not too ugly in the age of women's lib. Any of these liberated gals ever ask you?"

"Very few," Mark replied. "Look, there was a reason why I stopped by."

"Shoot, but if it has to do with the plant, forget it. It's Saturday night."

"I just got to thinking today, after I got that note, you know."

"Yeah," Bob said.

"Something Stuart Bennett said, not long after I came to work. I talked with him some. He's a pretty sharp old boy, if he's sober. I figured I could learn from him. Frank, you know, he was sort of cold, always uptight, hard to talk to. So Stu and I got pretty chummy and one day we were talking about something Frank had done and Stu said, 'You know, I'd like to see that son of a bitch realize his worst fear and splatter his ass on the concrete all the way from the top.'"

"Jesus," Bob said.

"I'd forgotten all about it, you know, with the shock of the accident and all, in taking over Frank's job." He paused, looked at Bob. "I'm not going to be able to keep it, am I?"

"I can't say, Mark. I don't fill the slots. I'm just a lowly start-up engineer."

"I can do the job," Mark said. "Frank taught me a lot. He knew his stuff. If he were alive and the job was open he'd say I could do it."

"What can I do?" Bob asked, spreading his hands.

"Tell them I can do it," Lingate said.

"There's one thing you'll learn in this business," Bob said after taking a sip of his drink, "and that's not to put your ass on the line for anyone unless you know what you're talking about. If I'd been working with you, Mark, and if I felt you could do the job, I wouldn't hesitate to put in a word for you. But I haven't been, and I don't know what you can do."

"Yeah, well, I can understand that," Mark said. He glanced at Tusk, who was watching how Mark Lingate's too handsome face showed no sign of the emotions that must have been behind his asking Bob for a favor.

"Do you think there's anything to what Stu said?" Mark asked.

"What makes you think there should be?" Tusk asked. "I thought it was an accident."

"Well, you know, there's talk."

"Who's talking?" Bob asked.

"Oh, just guys on the job, pipe fitters. I've heard a couple of them say things are a lot smoother now that he's, ah, gone. They didn't like that last inspection, when he black-lined so many welds. There's some tough guys around."

"Hell," Bob said, "some of those guys probably mess up welds deliberately. They get the same pay doing them over, and it takes longer."

"Well, I was just thinking about it," Mark said. "I guess I had better run along."

"Now that you're here, you're going to stay," Bob said. "And you'll do your duty. Later, when the music starts, you pay for your barbecued ribs by dancing at least once with every old married woman here, make 'em feel young again."

Mark grinned. "Well, there's some I wouldn't mind reminding of their youth."

It was Saturday night, and it was a fine party, and there were fine people there, solid people, and good talk. The ribs were greasy, hot with genuine Mexican chilis, and delicious after a couple of martinis. Some had brought swimsuits, the bar was stocked with bottles carried in, kids were exiled, it being an adult night, and Lindy was beautiful, soft and dreamy in his arms when Bob started the music, old stuff, dance music with real trumpets and saxes. Some got a little too drunk, two fell into the pool with clothes on and others followed, and Mark earned his barbe-cued ribs by dancing with married women and a widow.

It was late. The party was thinning. Three couples were dancing on the cleared patio, a few more were in lawn chairs. The lights were limited to the glow of a few kerosene burners jammed into the grass, and as Lindy and Mark Lingate danced, down on the far end of the patio, he not holding her closely at all but looking into her face, Tusk leaned on the bar, sipped one too many, and didn't notice that Leigh Warren had come to his side.

"Don't be mad at him," she said. "He's so cute."

"I promise not to get violent," he said. "No fights."

"After all, he's done his duty, dancing with all us old married women."

"A duty that I've neglected," he grinned.

"I didn't mean to hint, but since I did." She raised her arms and they moved out onto the patio. She danced well.

"We used to laugh at Mark, the way he was always hanging around. Frank would look grim and kid Lindy about it, but I think he was amused, too."

"Young love?" Tusk asked.

"The young lad's first encounter with an older femme fatale," she said. "By the way, I hope I'm not having that effect on you?"

"You're devastating me," he said. "But I won't embarrass you. I'm a young man of honor."

"You ooze honor," she said. "Maybe you're too honorable for your own good. Look, I know some are saying that it's wrong, the—to quote—way you and Lindy are carrying on, but don't listen to them, and don't listen to any objections she might have. I know that girl, and she's a man's woman, Mr. G.W. Smith, and unless I've lost my common sense, you're the man for her. You don't look anything alike, but you remind me so much of Frank. There's the same tough hide over a warm heart."

"Ah, you've got my number," he said as the dance ended, but her remark disturbed him. He and Frank had grown up in like circumstances, in the same small town. He didn't like the thought that Lindy was just seeing in him some of the characteristics, some of the speech patterns, that he had shared with Frank. He didn't like to think that his preoccupation with Lindy was interfering with his job. He didn't like himself too much.

He drank one too many, felt that fine edge of coordination just slightly impaired, and it was unusual for him. When your life can depend on quick moves, on undulled reflexes, you don't dull them with booze, not even on a pleasant

Saturday night in the company of fine people, all
of whom look as if murder would be the last
thing they'd do on this earth. But he kept remembering what Anna had said. "Work is the
likely place to meet a man." Most of those who
were present and had been present at the party
worked at the site.

He caught a glimpse of Lindy, still looking up at
Mark Lingate, talking seriously. No smiles. He
wondered what they were saying, tried to put
Mark in the picture that had, throughout the
evening, recurred to him: Lindy with her lover.
Mark Lingate didn't fit. He was too pretty, too
young. When the music ended it was the end of
an album side, and after the amplified click of
rejection there was a silence. Bob, laughing with
others in lawn chairs, made no move to get up to
change the record. Tusk thanked Leigh, saw
Lindy coming toward him.

"Time to go," she said.

What would he talk about, alone with her?
"One more drink," he said with a lopsided grin.

She got it. They moved off the patio, walked,
came abreast of the pool. "The water looks de-
lightful," she said.

He put an arm around her and pretended he
was going to throw her in. "Go ahead," he said.
She squealed and he held her close, feeling the
warmth of her.

"You wouldn't," she said.

"No."

Her smile was radiant, then mischievous. "*I* would," she said, shoving mightily. He caught her as he fell, and they tumbled in together, surfacing, Lindy laughing, he laughing with her as water streamed down her face. Her sodden hair clung to her finely shaped head.

"Kiddies, kiddies," Bob said, a little slurry, standing above them wagging a finger.

They had come in Lindy's Scout, and drove home with the wind drying their clothing, left a trail of damp garments. No more questions. No more doubts. She was in his arms.

11

Now it was a matter of waiting. The wheels were turning. Almost everyone alive in the United States is contained, somewhere, in a set of papers. If a man has served in the armed forces there is a file of information about him. If, as in the case of Bob Warren, he has at one time worked in sensitive areas of the services and has been cleared for secret material, the file can be extensive. In the past two decades, with more and more evidence of union corruption surfacing, no fewer than three government agencies, and in many cases some state agencies, have information on union leaders from the top down to the regional level. And all over the country, in the files of credit bureaus, banks, schools attended, places worked, there are tidbits of each individual's life on record.

That most of these sources are confidential is taken for granted by the average American. A man's bank account, for example, is promised to be a matter known only to himself and the bank's computer. Yet on a minor scale it is possible to estimate a man's checking account by picking up a telephone.

"This is Joe Jones, down at the Ford dealership. I have a check for two thousand three hundred dollars from Mr. Ronald Roe. Will his checking account cover it?"

The bank employee won't tell you the amount of cash in the checking account, but she or he will say, without hesitation, that Mr. Roe's account will or will not cover a check in the amount named.

Tusk knew from experience that the organization's ability to delve into the private lives of individuals came to multiples of the ingenious diggings of some inventive private detective, had often been astounded at what could be produced on short notice. Once, soon after he'd joined the organization—and he still wasn't one hundred percent sure why he'd been selected by the organization, a man with no feet, trying hard to adjust to the artificial feet in a veterans' hospital—he'd received information that could have come only from the big computers of the CIA.

Tusk suspected that he'd been recommended by the general, his old friend, for the organization had powerful friends, men who were sick of the miscarriages of justice, angry to see the victims of crime suffer while the criminals were housed and fed by the taxpayer. If any one man knew the human resources of the organization, it

could be the man who spoke in a hoarse, whispery, disguised voice. Tusk knew that a case in
North Carolina had been directed toward the
organization by a former federal judge, a man
who was highly respected throughout the entire
country. He'd learned that by accident, and he
would never mention it to anyone. He knew that
on each assignment he was given a police contact
if he requested one, so it was easy to imagine
how much effort went into that. The entire operation took time, manpower, money; from the executive jet with the permanently blacked-out
windows that carried him in for his personal
reports from some small airfield, to the speed
with which the organization delivered material
from the files of the bureaucracy, business and
local records.

He'd been doubtful at first. At first it looked
like vigilantism, looked as if men were taking the
law into their own hands. The organization was
not revolutionary, far from it. It was, if anything,
idealistic, anachronistic, using its resources to
return to a more primitive and more sure form of
justice based on the concept of the biblical laws.
An eye for an eye. If a man kills in cold blood, he
has forfeited the right to live. It was as simple as
that. It was impossible, however, to mete out justice in every case. The organization tended to
operate, through its field people such as Tusk
and the only other operative he knew, the
woman called Zed, in areas where police re-

sources were limited, where there was little likelihood of the killer's being caught and punished, even with the slap-on-the-wrist justice that often saw murder earn a mere seven years of prison.

Cases were selected, it seemed, by referral only, the client who paid talking to only one person, such as the ex-federal judge in North Carolina, never knowing, if the case was handled properly, that the ultimate punishment was anything more than a fortuitous accident.

And someone always paid—not enough to meet the expense of some operations, but a significant amount.

Tusk knew that ordinarily the death of his friend, Frank Pitt, would never have come to the attention of the organization. In an area of severely impacted crowding that overworked all police agencies, it would have been written off as an accident, even if someone like Bob Warren had suspected differently. In a way, the organization was elitist; its work was, by necessity, rarely publicized. When, as in the Arizona case, a woman was raped and mutilated, and years later a man died in punishment for the crime, the newspapers reported another accident, if a body was found; or another unsolved murder, if the operative was unskillful or unlucky in the completion of his assigned final task. And yet down in the bowels of society, in the underworld, among the carnivores who prey on society, a whispering campaign had begun years back, an intangible thing, a hint, a threat. A man might comment on the odd coincidence that a murderer who had drowned his victim died himself by drowning; wonder about it, make an offhand speculation that maybe there was some force out there that didn't like particularly brutal murders, didn't like murderers at all, believed in an eye for an eye.

Tusk thought he had come to accept his position long past, but during the days when he waited, days made to seem short by the wonder of loving a woman who loved him in return, he found himself dreaming at night, tossing in his bed, seeing his past, seeing the dead, seeing the face of a murderer who recognized at the last moment that he was to die, and found within himself a new area of doubt.

"Where would you like to live?" he asked Lindy, in one of the more pleasant moments of that waiting period.

"In your pocket," she said. "Make me small and carry me with you everywhere."

"Do you like boats?"

"Love them. Do you have one?"

"It isn't much of a boat. I like it. It's roomy. It's slow, but it gets there. I wouldn't want to take it into any big water, but we can tour the Keys and the Tortugas and the waterways up the east coast."

"Let's go now, tonight," she whispered.

"Do you want to keep this house?"

"Only if you want to live in it with me."

"Sell it, I think."

"Do we need the money?" she asked.

"No."

"Who are you, G.W.? What do you do? Why don't you need money?"

"Oh, I'm a saver," he said. "I put what I'd accumulated into a land development with some friends. They're doing well, and I get a cut of each lot they sell, each house. I have retirement and disability pay. If you're particularly demanding, I can always drive a nail or two, or do some commercial fishing."

"I have all I want," she said, clinging to him. "We'll stay together all day, all night, every hour, every minute, and I won't let you out of my sight."

He raised himself on one elbow to look down at her. "No nights out with the boys?" he grinned.

"One night every three months," she said. "I've always been alone. I don't like it."

"Even with Frank?"

"He had his work. When they were ready to put a plant on the line, or when they were behind, which was always, he'd be working seven twelves, twelve hours seven days a week. The money would roll in and I'd just be lonelier." She snuggled closer. "He asked me to get some counseling once. I did. We decided on the first visit, the shrink and I, that I was basically insecure."

"Are you?"

"I suppose so. Oh, there's no sad tale of childhood deprivation; I was lucky, actually. My dad was a television executive. I had a good home. I was loved. But I've never been happy alone. I quit going to the shrink because he was beginning to suggest that my problem was that I didn't like myself. I don't think he was right. Not that I'm in love with Lindy Pitt. I think I like her well enough, but I guess I'm shallow. She's not good company. I enjoy reading much more when...." She paused. "I was about to say when I can look up and see a man, but I guess I mean *my* man. And that's awkward as hell, because I've had two men, G.W. Frank and you. Before I went to work out at the plant I'd spend the hours keeping this place shining. It was so clean it almost hurt. If a grain of sand hit the carpet from Frank's shoes I'd be after it with a whisk broom or the vacuum. I polished the plumbing under the sinks. I dusted the ceiling twice a week."

"Well, if you like closeness, I can't think of any better way of life than living on a boat."

"It sounds wonderful. Let's go tonight."

"It won't be long," he promised.

He had never felt better. One day at the plant there was even some work to do, and he got into it, working in the sun, feeling the muscles respond, loosen. His body seemed to hum like a well-oiled machine. He felt something like an in-

ner glow, an overwhelming feeling of well-being,
and he tended to smile a lot, a big sandy-haired
man with not a few marks on his face going
around with a happy little canary-eating grin,
joking with his fellow workers, showing a will-
ingness that endeared him to the foremen and
dispatchers.

Three days after his initial request to Oscar, he
called again. He was informed that some material—of some interest, Oscar hinted—was on the
way by messenger service, should arrive within
twenty-four hours.

He could feel it coming to an end. Oscar's hint
told him that there was something significant in
the material that was coming, and he considered
staying home to wait for it. But if he went to
work, he could sneak down and see Lindy, for
she was assigned to gate duty that week.

At the construction shack he was told to report
to a start-up man named Bennett, somewhere up
top. That took in a lot of territory. He carried his
tools and got into an elevator, asked if anyone
knew where Stuart Bennett's crew was working.
No one knew. He went all the way to the top.
The welders were still at work on the core jacket,
but otherwise the top level was empty. He took
the time to look down and think a little. Two
levels down a crane protruded out into the open
space, cable reaching down, down, and far below
men were attaching the hook of the crane to a
crated piece of equipment. As he watched the

crate began to rise; the workers below scurried out from under. He started down, found Bennett on the level with the crane.

Crated equipment was protected by wood, wood had nails in it, and wood and nails called for a carpenter. His job was to knock the crates apart, carefully. Some of the equipment was delicate instrumentation. A crew with a forklift was working in conjunction with the crane. Bennett, looking as if he might have had a rough night, was directing placement of the crates before they were removed from the gear inside, then telling the forklift crew where to place the gear.

It wasn't the most rewarding work, waiting for a crate to be lifted up the equipment hatch from hundreds of feet below, using a pry lever and a band cutter to remove the wood, stacking the wood to one side, and there was plenty of time between crates to have a smoke, a cup of coffee. He tried to engage Bennett in conversation, but the man was all business, taking the job seriously. Everyone had a coffee break and the job went on and then it was lunchtime. Tusk declined an invitation from a young tech to go down and outside to eat in the fresh air. He found a seat on a piece of equipment encased in painted metal of a thickness that wouldn't be dented by his weight, and poured iced tea from his thermos. The rest of the crew went off toward the elevators, Stuart Bennett with them. He could hear the silence begin to fall over the plant, engines stopping, the crane operation on his level already gone, having left the last crate lifted, still attached to the cable, sitting on the floor.

He didn't mind being alone. He had Lindy to think about, the sweet and vulnerable Lindy, wanting only to be with him always. And his sandwiches were pretty good, made better by nips from a fresh chili. Funny you could find the real things this far north, probably, he thought idly, because of all the Mexican farm laborers around. Nothing has quite the flavor of a real Mexican chili pepper. If they'd make an ice cream with that flavor someone would get rich. Lindy liked them, too, could manage the real chili made by a chubby and friendly little Mexican woman in a joint over in Midland. And she liked fishing and swimming and was looking forward to learning scuba diving in the brilliant and warm waters off the Keys.

He finished his meal, lighted up. Lay back on the metal case, legs bent at the knees, feet hanging over the edge. A heaviness, pleasant, warm. Not that he was complaining, but a certain lady seemed to be causing him to lose a lot of sleep. Nice work. They'd have the rest of their lives to sleep in late, or, as it usually was aboard a boat, going to bed with the sun and rising with it. Privacy making it unnecessary to confine love to darkness hours. Wry thought. Good union carpenter having a little snooze on his lunch hour,

feeling the good, warm drowsiness that is there
only when you're taking a nap at some unexpected time, never at bedtime. Lindy smiling.
Lindy in that bikini. And from far off the sound
of an engine, boat engine, the old *Duck*, have to
change the name. Something cute for Lindy. Engine louder. No boat. He opened his eyes, still
half out of it, started to sit up. It was the crane
engine. Operator back early from lunch. The
cable taut, lifting the crate still attached to it,
crate swinging.

A drowsy little nap and thoughts of Lindy and
the crate swinging his way, too fast before alarm
triggered his reaction, the crate, heavy, encased
in wood, coming toward him fast, just off the
floor, at the height of the piece of gear on which
he was lying. He sat up fast but not fast enough,
still in that haze of sleep and thoughts of Lindy,
and the crate smashed in, wood cracking, catching his feet just at the top edge of the metal case.
His leather work shoes and plastic feet were
crunched in, and smashed, pinned there. There
was a sharp pain in his left leg as the distortion of
his artificial feet caused straps to be pulled too
tight.

He tried to jerk free, but the crate was heavy,
the instrument case on which he sat jammed
tightly against a wall. The cable was loosening,
and as he bent to start unbuckling, to get away
from the crunched feet trapped between the two
heavy objects, he realized that there was one

helluva fine operator working that thing, for
with a few little jerks and some manipulation,
the hook slid out of the looped chains around the
crate, drew away, swung, lowered. The buckles
of his harness were digging into his flesh, too
tight.

It took the crane operator three tries to snag
the hook into the latticed metal braces of a
heavy piece of equipment and begin to lift.
Metal scraped and grated; the lifted ton or so of
equipment tilted, banged the floor, began to
rise. He broke a fingernail trying to open the
buckles, cursed himself, watched as the heavy,
deadly metal mass rose high and started to
swing his way, had his hand in his pocket. A
good carpenter always carries a pocketknife. He
forced himself to look away from the swinging
mass, concentrated, one slash, two. Straps cut.
Skin of a tender stump being lacerated as he
jerked one leg free, giving an upward glance. It
was almost overhead, high as the high ceiling
would allow, another strap and then the last
and it was coming, gears and wheels screaming
as the mass was dropped, still hooked to the
crane cable, coming down too fast, too damned
fast, as he threw himself off and away, hit the
floor on his shoulder with a jar that he didn't
feel as he rolled and heard the smashing, tearing
sounds behind him, still rolling as the falling
mass bounced, smashed the spot where he'd
been sitting, came rolling after him as he came up

with a jar against metal and could go no farther.

It stopped just short of him. Then he felt the protest of the pain in his shoulder, even as he leaped to his knees, still holding the knife, knee-walked as fast as he could toward the crane. He heard the clang of work shoes on metal, the thud of a man making the last few feet to the floor in a leap, ignored the pain in his knees as he scrambled around the tracks of the crane.

He saw nothing, heard only the sound of running footsteps diminishing.

The cuts on the tender stump were superficial. His shoulder was only bruised. The hurting, he felt, was worth it, because he was so close now that he could smell it. And things were becoming clear now. Someone had dropped a bundle of welding rods on Frank and, missing, had found another way to kill, and that someone knew that he was now being hunted. That narrowed the field considerably. The man who had killed Frank had tried to kill him. That man was one fine crane operator.

He was knee-walking slowly back to take a look at his feet, still jammed between the two masses, when two of the crew came back, looked at the smashed equipment, ventured a "What the hell!" while watching him as he knee-walked to try to jerk the smashed feet out.

"What the hell is going on here?" Stuart Bennett asked, coming up behind the gawking men who were watching Tusk.

Oh, God damn, yes, he was getting close. How many people knew he was working in that exact location?

"Damned if I know, Bennett," he said. "I was having a little nap and some joker started playing with the crane. He didn't seem to know what the hell he was doing, and the first thing I knew he was losing control and I moved just in time."

"Oh, hell," Bennett said. "It'll take two hundred pages in triplicate to report this."

"Bennett," Tusk said. "I've got a spare set of feet down in my van on the parking lot. You wanna send someone down for me?"

"Sure, sure, and then you'll have to make a report."

"Just get the feet, then we'll worry about a report," he said.

One of the crewmen volunteered. Tusk gave him his key and instructions as to where to find the feet. He answered questions, repeated basically the same thing. He'd been having a nap, and someone had started playing with the crane. Stuart Bennett was curiously quiet, the questions coming from the other workers and the young techs. Abe Johnson, start-up supervisor, came hurrying up. Tusk had seen him around, having had him pointed out by Bob Warren, but he had not yet had an opportunity to speak with him. He was a man tending to show his age in a protruding stomach, sagging neck, balding head. He wore a business suit that was slightly wrinkled, as if worn three or four days in a row, and he was breathing hard.

A man who had run away in panic, after seeing his victim escape, would be breathing hard. But an old man hurrying to the scene of an accident would be breathing hard, too.

"I don't understand," Johnson said after hearing Tusk tell his story again. "No one would just be *playing* with a crane. Sounds to me as if someone was doing it deliberately."

"I don't know," Tusk said. "Maybe just having his kicks, scaring the shit out of a carpenter."

The young tech came back with Tusk's feet. He'd pulled himself up onto a crate to sit and now took the feet, strapped them on. They were dressed in old-fashioned penny loafers.

"You come with me, Smith," Abe Johnson said. "We'll have a nurse look at you."

"I'm fine," Tusk said.

"Just in case," Johnson said firmly. Just in case you decide to file a claim, he was saying. "Get this mess cleaned up," Johnson said to Bennett. "Get me a report on the damage before quitting time."

The nurse in the first-aid station told him to remove his shirt, put a cold stethoscope to his back and chest, shook her head at the bruise on his shoulder, which was beginning to color, dappled some ointment on the scratches on his legs.

Tusk followed the supervisor through the start-up offices. "Sit down at the desk," Johnson said when they were in his private office. "I'd like for you to fill in the accident form while it's still fresh in your mind."

"Not much to tell," Tusk said. He looked at the form, wrote briefly, shoved it toward Johnson, who had taken the chair on the other side of the desk.

"You're sure that's all you can tell us?" Johnson asked.

"Maybe you can think of something," Tusk said, looking at Johnson with a grim little smile on his face. Close, God, yes, he was close. "What did Frank Pitt report about his near accident?"

"What do you mean?" Johnson asked, his face going white. "Near accident? The man was killed."

"I mean the one where he was almost hit by a bundle of welding rods."

"You have my attention." Johnson's hand was shaking slightly as he reached for a cigarette. "There was no report made to me about a near accident involving a bundle of welding rods."

"I wonder why, Mr. Johnson?" Tusk asked. "Could it have been, perhaps, that he thought you might already know about it?"

The hand that flicked a Bic lighter was shaking noticeably. "I think I know who you are," Johnson said.

"Tell me."

"You've been sent here to investigate Pitt's

death," Johnson said. "I've been expecting someone, but I think the company could have done me the courtesy of telling me, since I was the one who requested an investigation."

"I work alone," Tusk said, taking on the role assigned to him by Johnson, very interested now. "Did you put your request in writing?"

"Of course. If you'll excuse me. It's right there in the desk."

Tusk changed chairs with him, Johnson finding a manila envelope quickly, removing a letter. It was worded in businessese, with even a "whereas" thrown in, and the gist of it was, as Johnson implied, a request to the utility's home office to institute an investigation into the death of one Frank Pitt, start-up engineer.

"What made you first think that it was not a simple accident?" Tusk asked, shoving the letter back.

"He had no reason to be topside," Johnson said. "I know. I know what he was working on. Some of the younger men may think that I don't know my job. Pitt, in fact, was one of them. But I make it my business to know what my engineers are doing, Mr. Smith. He had no reason to go up there that evening. He was deathly afraid of heights, and he wouldn't have gone just to see the sights."

"He had a telephone call, Mr. Johnson. He was asked to go up there."

"You're sure?" Johnson asked, reaching for

another cigarette. "Jesus, I was afraid of something like that."

"Do you have any idea who might have wanted Frank Pitt dead?" Tusk asked.

"I know what you might be thinking, Mr. Smith," Johnson said, lighting his cigarette. "You may even have seen some of the detrimental reports that young Pitt submitted over my head regarding me and how I handle my job. You're thinking that I had a reason, aren't you?"

"He was trying to get you fired," Tusk said.

"Yes," Johnson said. "What Pitt didn't know was that I was actively trying to be removed from this job. In fact, I'd requested that I be replaced, and that Frank Pitt be named as assistant supervisor in charge of start-up."

"Do you—"

"In writing," Johnson said, beginning to regain his composure. He fished out two letters. One was a carbon, the other an original, on company letterhead, formally denying his request to be transferred and stating that the management had decided Frank Pitt was not yet ready to be placed in so responsible a position. The dates of the letters preceded Frank's death by some weeks.

"Does that remove me from your list of suspects, Mr. Smith?" Johnson asked.

It didn't, not entirely. "I don't think you were ever seriously considered, Mr. Johnson," Tusk said. "And now that circumstances have, ah, unmasked me, I might be calling on you for help."

"If there's anything at all I can do," he said. "I am interested in my men, Mr. Smith. I've been in this work all my life, and I've seen bright young men come and go, and I can remember when I was like them. I do my best to help them along in their careers. We need good men in this industry, heaven knows. Frank Pitt's death was especially unfortunate, since he had quite a bright future. Whatever some may think, I am not jealous of my authority. I've earned it, and my record with this company is good. Even if I can't spout figures and outslide-rule the younger men, even if I don't know all there is to know about nuclear reactors, I do know how to manage men. That's my job. Theirs is to know the technology and to do the actual work. I bore Pitt no real ill will. He angered me at times, for he was quite unreasonable. He was ambitious, and he thought he could get my job by showing that I was not as bright as some newly graduated nuclear engineer. But I am as interested as you in discovering what happened."

"Thank you, Mr. Johnson," Tusk said. "I may be calling on you. In the meantime, let me ask you once more: can you think of anyone who might have had good reason for wanting Frank dead?"

"No, no, not at all. Oh, there was some friction between Frank and some of the contractors, between him and the unions. He was unreasonable about the unions, too. He irritated a lot of people."

"Like Ernest Martin?"

"Yes, he had his problems with Martin. But I can't envision Martin as a killer. His power is secure. Pitt was no more than a minor irritation to him."

"One more question, Mr. Johnson. You tumbled to me rather quickly. What made you think I was here to look into Pitt's death?"

"I was informed quite early that you were not merely a carpenter—I'd rather not say by whom."

"I'd rather you did say," Tusk said mildly. "Don't force me to go above this office to get you to say."

"It was one of the start-up engineers, a friend of Pitt's."

"Let's not be coy," Tusk said.

"All right, damn it, but please don't let him know I told you. He's clearly above suspicion, being Pitt's best friend, with their wives good friends, as well."

"Bob Warren?" Tusk asked, not really believing it.

"Yes. He felt that I should know, in the event of trouble. I've managed to establish a good working relationship with young Warren. Please don't do anything to disrupt it."

"I'll respect your confidence," Tusk said, rising.

He was close. The murderer had made his move. Whoever it was, he'd be panicky now, and from here on in he wouldn't be facing a lovesick man reverting to childhood.

But Bob Warren, a stoolie for the supervisor whom Frank had labeled as totally incompetent? Curious. Very curious.

12

THERE WAS NO REAL REASON to finish out his shift. He avoided questions in the construction shack. Word of an accident traveled fast. He beat the evening traffic by a couple of hours, saw Anna Larch sitting in her rocker on the front porch. She waved to him as he parked in the driveway, and called out that she had something for him.

"It came by messenger," she said. "When I told him you weren't here he said that a Mrs. Anna Larch was authorized to sign for it."

She extended a manila envelope, plain, no return address. "You see, Anna," he grinned, "I trust you."

"Well, I *almost* opened it."

"You wouldn't do a thing like that."

"Coffee? Or a beer?"

"No, thanks," he said. "I have some reading to do."

In his room he tossed the packet onto the bed, had a wash, removed his feet and rubbed an antiseptic salve on his scratched stump, sat Indian fashion on the bed. A handwritten note was atop. Oscar's handwriting.

"Complete with one exception. Expect remainder within seventy-two hours." The note was initialed "O."

He leaned over and snagged a beer, opened it. It was a moment to be savored, not to be rushed into. In the one-inch-thick stack of Xerox papers he held could be not only the key but the answer. Each of the individual reports had a cover sheet with the name of the subject typed in the center of an otherwise blank page. He arranged them in an order that presented itself in his mind, for he had, in theory, eliminated some of the people involved.

BARDONI, ANGELO. Born. . . .

Tusk skimmed. Bardoni was a Pennsylvanian. He was married and had three children. He'd served in the marines during the Nam thing, two tours in the jungles. Held a bronze star. You can never tell by looking at a man.

He had two arrests on his record, both for public drunkenness and brawling. He was Mr. Middle Industrial America. He owned a mortgaged home, a mortgaged car, a mortgaged pickup truck. He had worked all over the United States since Nam, and had once done a six-month contract on the North Sea. His income-tax file showed that a pipe fitter makes one helluva lot of money. His credit record showed that he spent it all and more. Midland police had made a call to

the Bardoni home back in December, on a complaint from the neighbors, but an obviously
bruised Mrs. Bardoni had refused to press
charges. There was nothing in the report, complete as it was, that changed Tusk's opinion of
Bardoni.

WARREN, ROBERT B.

Six-year hitch, navy. Nuclear technician
aboard a guided-missile destroyer. Good-conduct
medal. Asian theater medals. No arrests. Cleared
"confidential" while in the navy. Tech school.
Marriage. Kids. Income—less than Bardoni's.
House mortgage. Car paid for. Savings account.
Mr. Solid America. Conservative. Registered
Republican. Wife former—aged—Age of children. Wife's background, Indiana. Nothing out of
the ordinary.

LINGATE, MARCUS W.

Incomplete. This was not unusual. He was on
his first job, was too young to have been drafted.
The system was just beginning to absorb the vital
statistics of Mark Lingate into its files and computers. Rental apartment. Mortgaged car, sporty.
Mortgaged four-wheeler. Personal investigation
going backward from Cal. Tech, where he was an
honors graduate, tops in his class, Engineers'
Club, Drama Club, no arrests, no convictions, no
real paper personality yet. Too young. Reason for
delay, no immediate family, parents dead.

JOHNSON, ABRAHAM P.

Age nearing sixty-five. Family man, two

daughters and two sons, all married, ten grandchildren. One job in his entire life, with Tips.
Worked up from the bottom to become supervisor, then executive. Home in Boise, paid for,
valued at more than one hundred thousand.
Rental apartment in Petertown. Wife sixty-one,
health frail. No outstanding debts. Savings com-
patible with a man, a thrifty man, who drew a
good salary and had done so for the past twenty
years, after advancing beyond the stage of labor-
er. Personal friends included top executives of
Tips. No arrests. Church member. Lions Club.
Board of directors, Chamber of Commerce. Solid
Upper-Middle America.

BENNETT, STUART O.

Not as old as he looked. Master's degree in
Electrical Engineering from Ohio State. Twice
married, twice divorced. Paying child support for
one girl still underage. A reasonable figure not
incompatible with his income, which was just
below that of Bob Warren. Lived alone in rental
apartment. Behind in his payments to the telephone company, and on a year-old car; often late
with his rent. One arrest and conviction for
drunken driving with revocation of license for
two years, revocation time since expired. Had
worked a variety of jobs since leaving the plant
where he had panicked and done some damage.
Income-tax report audited, with underpayment
made, plus interest and penalties, 1976. Audited
regularly each year since. No more offenses.

Known to be a habitual drinker. Stateside service with Army Engineer Corps during Korean War. No distinctions, no black marks. One ex-wife had remarried, the mother of the underage child. The other had not demanded alimony, was living alone in Florida on her own money.

One by one the reports, which he skimmed quickly, seemed to confirm his opinions. He had saved the best for the last, and now reached for another beer, settled down to do more than skim the last report, well, the next to the last, but the report labeled PITT, BELINDA (Mrs. Frank) was not properly a part of the package. He had ordered it on a whim. He felt a little guilty about it, as he tossed it to one side. It was like spying on her in secret. And yet he knew he would read it, because she was going to be a part of his life from now on. Maybe he'd show it to her one day and they'd laugh about it. Maybe he could say, "Don't ever tell me a fib, because I've got your entire life on paper." No. He wouldn't. He would toss it aside, burn it. More fun to learn about her in person, in the flesh. Now why the hell did he have to put it that way, take his mind off the biggie that he'd saved to the last? Daydreaming about Lindy had almost cost him his life up there in the reactor building.

MARTIN, ERNEST.

Born San Francisco, only nine years of school, work on the Frisco docks, arrested at seventeen for assault in strike dispute, conviction suspended on good behavior. Union organizer, North Pacific Coast area; two arrests in Portland, no convictions, both arrests involving strike activity.

No skimming this one. He read it carefully as a man's life began to form, a tough dock kid quick with his fists or a blackjack, learning quickly that there was less labor and more money available for a man who used his head instead of his back, working as a stevedore for only two years before moving into the organizing end of the labor movement. When he was twenty-four he'd switched his affiliations from stevedores' unions to construction unions, where, during the Korean War, there was vast opportunity for a young man willing to do anything.

Surprisingly, Martin had been in the area for a long time. He owned a three-hundred-thousand-dollar house and ranch outside of Petertown and had four children, ages ranging from postcollege to a teenager at home.

Surprisingly, too, he was not the head of the local pipe-fitters union, but merely a sort of second man, an assistant in name, but in actuality the moving power. He could single-handedly bring vast projects to a halt. No man got a card without Martin's approval. No contractor used pipe fitters without dealing with Martin. He had a lot of power.

And now there was some skipping, over a long list of union actions involving Martin's local. But he forced himself not to read ahead to the meaty parts, studied the financial reports. Income-tax returns in perfect order, prepared by a C.P.A. Investment programs involving mainly real estate, an income in six figures from lease of irrigated farming and fruit acreage.

Martin was not poor, would not even miss his salary from the union if it should be stopped. Curious. Safety-deposit boxes in three banks, contents not checked, but known to consist of gold in coin form, purchase records copied, amounts in the five-figure range when gold was below two hundred. The man was certainly not hurting.

Member of a local Catholic church, member of the Kiwanis and Lions Clubs, not active in either.

And then a new wrinkle. A page turned. A sealed envelope attached to the next page. Written neatly on the envelope in Oscar's hand, "Read and destroy immediately." He opened it.

The name of a bank in Zurich, a number, a figure.

Tusk whistled, for two reasons. New respect for the organization, for one thing. He'd never guessed that they had the ability to reach into that haven of secrecy, the Swiss banking system. For another reason, the figure with a dollar sign in front of it, two million five. Even. On the button.

He burned the envelope and contents in a large ashtray, went back to the report, more certain

than ever that Martin was his man. He found
more financial matters, part ownership of a
casino in Las Vegas, and that caused a little
prickle of something on the back of his neck.
He'd always wondered what would happen if the
organization came head to head with the Mafia.
If that was going to happen here he hoped old
Oscar and the people back there in the East had
the cavalry ready.

And then the capper. One by one the company
names he'd given Oscar by telephone, and one by
one figures that explained the two-point-five
million in the Swiss bank.

Martin was hitting one of the larger contractors
on the site for a cool two hundred grand a year,
just to keep his pipe fitters on the job, and that
two hundred thousand wasn't going into union
coffers. He was simply putting the arm on every
contractor on the list, big hits for the big boys, little hits for the small ones.

And Frank Pitt had written in his notebook,
"*Get* Martin's ass *tomorrow*." Then he fell. And
Frank was a nosy fellow, not satisfied unless he
knew all there was to know about the job he was
working on.

The scenario wrote itself. Frank worked with
both union and contractors, a cohesive force, one
of his duties to keep peace between the testy
union and the contractors who saw their profit
margins threatened. Martin was trying to bleed
the company, and Frank wasn't about to allow it.

What would Frank have done? Abe Johnson
had said that Frank didn't understand the
unions, so he wouldn't have gone through them.
He probably wouldn't have gone to Abe. Go over
Abe's head? Possibly. But it was more in Frank's
character to go straight to Martin, tell him that
he had the goods on him, threaten to blow the
whistle unless Martin stopped his bleeding of the
contractors and left the company alone.

Damn it, Frank, why didn't you write down
why you were seeing Martin? But it was there.
There was the profit, the money. There in Ernest
Martin's pocket. There wasn't enough to convict
Martin of murder, but there was enough to send
him off for quite a few years as a labor racketeer.
That wouldn't quite cut it, however. If Martin
had given Frank his fatal shove there was only
one answer to it: that someone give Martin a fatal
shove.

He felt a sense of satisfaction. He had known
he was close, and now there remained only one
last thing. He had to prove his suspicions. Fortunately, he was not bound by the rules of evidence, by the code of justice that seemed more
intent on protecting the criminal than on punishing him. He had only five men to convince of
Martin's guilt: himself, first, and then the judge,
the prosecutor, the coordinator, the man without
a name. He knew exactly how he would do it, for
in questioning a man he was not required to read
him his rights, not required to be polite or gentle.

Soon Frank's death would be balanced on the scales of a harsh sort of justice. Soon it would be over. He'd been instructed to inform Oscar when the end was near. He was too exposed, known by too many to be a friend of the dead man. He'd complicated things by falling in love with Frank's widow.

But, damn it, he wanted this one. This one was personal. He would handle it, because it didn't matter if his future effectiveness was impaired. He wasn't going to have a future with the organization. He had no contract. He did have an understanding that he could step out anytime he was ready, no obligations. And since things might just get a bit hectic in the next day or so, and since he did owe the organization, he decided to inform them of his plans, at least in part.

He was a man who believed in doing first things first. There was still Lindy's file to be read, if he didn't decide to play fair with her and burn it. That, however, was something that could be decided later. He went out onto the porch. Anna was working in the backyard, an old-fashioned sun bonnet hiding her face. He went into the cluttered living room and had Oscar on the telephone in seconds.

"Oscar," he said, "the job here is to be terminated in the next day or so, in a natural way, no problems."

"I understand, sir," Oscar said. "You will be

able to wait for the agreed-upon arrival of your gear?''

"No, we don't need the cavalry this time," Tusk said. "And Oscar, I want you to tell the board that this is my last trip."

"I beg your pardon, sir?"

"This is it, Oscar. The last. I'm going to go fishing."

"You seem upset, sir," Oscar said, pushing a button on his desk as he talked. In another room a light flashed, and a wheelchair moved soundlessly as a mutilated hand reached for a button that brought Tusk's voice into the room.

"Not at all," Tusk said. "The job went smoothly. The data you sent winds it up. Natural conclusion, no problems. No cavalry, and then I'm retiring. Don't call me and I won't call you."

"You will, sir, make the final report?"

"Not in person. I'll be getting married."

In the well-lighted building, doors opened, operated by scanners whose beams were broken by the movement of the soft-tired wheelchair. The voice was undisguised, flat, unaccented.

"Shall I send the message?" Oscar asked.

"As quickly as possible, if you please."

There was a silence as the long, irritating chore of getting an overseas line, of contacting the Jamaican operator, was accomplished. Another long wait while she was being paged, then the calm voice.

"How's the weather, Oscar?"

"Rather stormy, I fear."

"I was afraid of that."

"If you are quick about it, you'll be able, possibly, to keep your appointment in Manhattan," Oscar said.

"Damn."

"Very sorry," Oscar said, hanging up with a quizzical smile directed toward the man in the wheelchair. The mutilated face had long since ceased to pain him.

"I fear, sir," Oscar said, "that he's taking matters into his own hands. I feared this from the beginning, what with the personal element involved."

"He has served well," the man in the wheelchair said.

"He's been rather careless of late, however."

The man sighed. "He was the best we had."

"Perhaps he'll reconsider."

"No. I've seen it coming. If this affair is concluded to our satisfaction, I want you to send along a little bonus. A wedding present."

"It will be my pleasure," Oscar said, to the back of the retreating head.

13

HE PACED THE SMALL SPACE available in the room in Anna Larch's house, making his plans. There was an inner excitement, a knowing that the end of the hunt was near, a certainty that, he knew, was not based on the bedrock of sure knowledge, but was there nevertheless. Martin was tough, his past record showed that, but even the toughest have a breaking point when faced with the cold assurance of something bigger and crueler and meaner than themselves. He had dealt with tough ones before.

But he'd been wrong twice. All the evidence pointed straight to Martin. There was more than enough money involved to generate a murder, but what if once again he was wrong? What if he split Martin open and out spilled convincing proof that it was not Martin who had pushed Frank?

He reviewed the possibilities. Murder motives do not always have to involve huge sums of money. Murder can arise from quick passion. Bardoni. Murder can grow in a diseased mind from motives quite obscure, as unimportant as damaged pride. Stuart Bennett. The murder motive can be hidden deep inside a mind, so arcane that only luck or accident can reveal it. Not Bob Warren. Not Mark Lingate. And that left the casual possibilities, someone not in the picture, a worker who just didn't like Frank, a private grudge engendered by Frank's driving desire to see good work done.

If not Martin, who? And if not Martin, what then? Call it, after all, an accident? Forget that someone made a call to Frank and asked him, evidently, to come up to the top level of the reactor building?

It had to be Martin, and tomorrow was the day to find out. Tomorrow. Meanwhile there was the night. Lindy was expecting him. Lindy.

It was there on the bed, labeled PITT, BELINDA (MRS. FRANK).

It wasn't fair to use the resources of the organization to spy on her. It was something like sneaking into her bureau to see if she arranged her scanties neatly. But she was his, was to be his for the rest of their lives, and she had nothing to hide, had told him, in those long and whispery talk sessions, so much that he knew her better than he'd ever known another person.

With a shrug and a wry grin at himself, he sat on the edge of the bed. He'd just peek. That was all, just a peek.

PITT, BELINDA ALICE, (MRS. FRANK). Nee

BELINDA ALICE ECKHART. Former MRS. ARNOLD DORR.

Just a peek, and it hit him at the top of the page. The former Mrs. Arnold Dorr. He felt a quick surge of betrayal. Unreasonable. He threw the sheaf of paper from him, rose, lighted a cigarette. Not once had she mentioned that she'd been married before she met Frank. The old-fashioned girl, taking her virginity to the marital bed. But damned sure not Frank's.

But, damn it, so what? So she had chosen not to tell him. Perhaps it was not a pleasant memory. Maybe she hadn't even told Frank; at least Frank had never mentioned it. But why should he? And it had happened long ago, long before he knew that Lindy existed. She was still Lindy, and she'd come into his life long after he had a right to expect the young and trembling thrills that she gave him, something so tender, so precious, that he had no right to question anything about her.

Throw the damned thing in the wastebasket. Shred it. Forget he'd ever seen those words—the former Mrs. Arnold Dorr. Sooner or later she'd get around to telling him. She, too, was alone, hated to be alone, was scared to lose him, as if such a thing would change his opinion of her.

But it was there, and honor wearing thin, he once again picked it up.

G.W. Smith had not cried since he lost his dog when he was a boy. He hadn't cried when he awoke in a field hospital and discovered that he was missing his feet; not when his mother and father died, for they had lived good lives, useful lives, and had weathered a lot of good years. He didn't cry as he read hurriedly, discovering that the Belinda Pitt he had thought he knew was a more infinitely complicated girl than he'd ever suspected, remembering the things she had told him as he read, and knowing an ache of tenderness and pity that merely made his love for her stronger.

Belinda Eckhart, Brooklyn, New York. Mother Alice Eckhart, cocktail waitress, laundry worker, sometimes welfare recipient. Father John R. Eckhart, deceased, early.

"Oh, there's no sad tale of childhood deprivation; I was lucky, actually."

School and high school in Brooklyn. Summer and after-school work as a waitress in local restaurants.

There, between the lines of the cold facts collected by faceless people he would never know, was Lindy, alone, her mother working nights, hints of a drinking problem, a hearing when she was ten that narrowly missed calling Alice Eckhart an unfit mother. One unproven accusation of child abuse against the mother; denied by Lindy, who testified that she had fallen.

Work after high school, in a Manhattan department store, clerk, then in-house model. Night courses at N.Y.U. Good grades. Classes heavy in the drama and speech areas at other establishments. And he could see her, a young girl from Brooklyn, fighting the accent—coming, at last, to that almost unreal unaccented speech that is the mark of the TV commercial actress—fighting to learn the model's walk, the way of moving. Mother dying. Income during those years at the survival level. A daring move into free-lance modeling, the thoroughness of the organization illustrated by a copy of a newspaper ad showing Lindy, young and thin and lovely, in a tennis out-fit. No great success, but a move up in income. And then Arnold Dorr, buyer for an Orlando department store, ten years her senior; and then heartbreak, Orlando police reports, the first inci-dent resulting in no charges, the second resulting in a battered flaxen-haired girl being hospital-ized, divorce. Clerk in a Jacksonville ladies-wear store. Frank Pitt.

And that was her life. He burned, hated a man he'd never seen, felt an insane urge to go to Florida, find one Arnold Dorr. Instead he went to find Lindy.

"I thought hamburgers on the patio," she said, after a surprisingly hard and lingering kiss at the door, a kiss that made her feel warm inside, made her smile soft and smugly happy.

"Dessert?"

"The usual, buster—me."

He was looking at her with new eyes. She was so confident, so mature, so sophisticated. But in-side? He knew a great welling up of emotion, of warmth for her, loving pity, a promise that never again would she know unhappiness. He kissed her on the neck as she made meat patties for the burgers, was told to bug off and fix a drink if he didn't want dessert served first.

She was wearing a little summer frock, all whites and yellows, because he'd once remarked that she looked great in dresses, even the sacks that designers were forcing on women too stupid to reject them. She looked good in anything. And in a day or so they'd be off, leaving the house that Frank built in the hands of a realtor, off to the far coast where meandering waterways cut salt marshes and great white birds waded the tidal pools and gulls braked and flew low begging for tidbits behind a lazily moving boat.

"What is it with you?" she asked him.

"Why do you ask?"

"Something's going on. You're different."

Women made good investigators, inner barometers attuned to minor changes in mood, that eternal intuition. He grinned, thinking, I know you girl. I know you now. And I like you even better for what I know, for the pain you've felt, for giving me a chance to show you how much joy life can be. He wanted to blurt it out, to tell her what he'd done, how it made her seem dearer to him, more feminine, more worthy of protection and tenderness and love. But she'd chosen to hide that part of her life. He would never mention it. And if she should, he'd tell her that it

didn't matter, that the Belinda who existed
before she came to G.W. was another person, and
the only problem now was to make Belinda and
G.W. an entity.

Lots of onions, a touch of green chili pepper,
sweat forming at a bite, the tart hotness good in
the cool of a twilight scented by the damp, sweet
smell of newly mowed grass under sprinklers. He
told her fishing stories, how the northern-
population blues, influenced by some change in
current or temperature, came as far south as the
Frying Pan Shoals off the North Carolina coast in
the fall and winter; how one of the bruising,
fighting twenty-pounders on light tackle is not
only an hour's entertainment, but a baked meal
for two to six people. She pulled her chair close
so that their knees touched, and she leaned toward him in rapt attention, both of her soft
hands holding one of his. He talked for a long,
long time, and she, as if sensing that there was
something different in him, listened with only
small comments.

Later he went to sleep holding her close, his
arms protecting her from the slight chill that
crept in the open windows late at night, just as
he would protect her forever from a life that had
given her a handicap in the beginning. Not that
he considered her to be so weak, for she had,
after all, overcome a start in life that would have
defeated many, had taken the raw material of a
deprived childhood and turned it into something

exquisitely rare. He had shredded the report that had told him so much about her before coming to her house. He would never mention it. If at some time in the future she decided to tell him the truth, he would listen with understanding, tell her he understood. All of the things that had happened to her had gone into making up the Lindy he held in his arms. That end product was worth all that had gone into it.

Before sleep, in the warm aftermath of their love, he had told her that very soon now they'd be heading east. She did not question him, merely accepted it. He felt that she understood, without putting it into words, that balance would be restored, meaning that Frank's killer would be found and punished. That dark side of his life would never be thrust upon her, however. She would never know that he had, on occasion, with the proof undeniable, meted out eye-for-an-eye justice, that he intended doing it just once more. In a way it was a method of earning the goodness that he held in his arms. Frank had paid the ultimate price to open the way to his discovery that he was not too old, too hardened, to know total love. When he heard the admission from the lips of Frank's killer, when he made things right, then that debt would be paid.

For the first time he spent the entire night in her house. He had set an alarm, and when it went off she mumbled and protested and hid her face in the pillow, so he left her there. He had completed dressing and was about to walk out of the room.

"Darling," she said, voice morning-deep.

He sat on the edge of the bed. "I was going to give you a day off."

"No. Have to get to work."

"Stay in bed."

"Umm," she said, arching her back toward his touch.

"You might even start packing," he said.

She sat up, letting the sheets fall away. "Last night you made it sound as if today might be the last day."

"Well, who knows?"

"You're not going to—ah, do anything, ah, silly?"

"Who? Me?"

"You talked about everything. Everything but that," she said. "You've told me all about yourself, and nothing. I've been putting it all together. Frank said you were in some kind of investigative work, he thought. You told me that Frank's death was not an accident. And now you seem so sure that this is going to be our last day here, tell me to start packing. I'm frightened."

"No need. I have some ideas. If they work out, then I'll just call in the police." Another indiscretion. An admission of his mission. But this was Lindy. "You stay in bed for a while. Get up and start sorting out what you'll need immediately. We'll have movers in for the other stuff. Or we can come back later and sort it all out."

"Darling, can't we just forget? Nothing will change the fact that he's dead." She clung to him. "You stay in bed, too. We'll get up later and give a lot of things to the Salvation Army and call in this realtor I know and then—"

"Tomorrow, or the next day."

14

HE DID NOT REPORT to the construction shed. He went into the reactor building, rode the elevator to the top. The crew working on the jacket at the top level was in the process of tool setup. He stayed out of sight until they had gone behind their plastic-shrouded shield and the welding torches were hissing. It was the symbolic place, the logical place. He found a telephone on the in-plant system and called a number that he'd obtained in advance. The union had an office in the plant. A woman who sounded as if she had not had a good night's sleep told him that Mr. Martin was not yet in the office. Yes, he was expected, but he didn't usually get in until after ten.

He found a crew with a coffee urn on a mid level and killed twenty minutes, then decided to check out the way down, going back topside, making his way down the stairwells mounted against the outside walls. He met a few men coming up, walking one or two flights of stairs instead of waiting for the elevator. He wasn't concerned about being seen. There were more than fifteen hundred men on the job at the site. He had his identification badge. It was just a matter of looking as if he knew where he was going.

He had a smoke outside. Behind him the plant's PA system came to life. "All right, electricians' local—" he missed the number "—hit the gate. All electricians hit the gate." A wobble. Soon men began streaming out of the plant, going into the parking lots, standing around. He, still having time to kill, fell in with a group and climbed into the van. With the lot full of electricians waiting to see the outcome of the wobble he was just one among many. A few of the men took advantage of the wobble to have a day off, getting in cars and driving away.

Waiting didn't bother him. However, when the PA system, the voice coming to the parking lot over outside speakers, came to life again, a voice sounding very much like Ernest Martin's telling all pipe fitters to hit the gate, he sat up straight in the seat and with a frown on his face watched pipe fitters come out of the plant.

But he'd seen a couple of wobbles of the type that was going on. They were usually quickly settled. The day was young, and if work was shut down then the chances were good that there'd be no one on the top level. He had a cup of coffee from his thermos. Eleven o'clock came and no change. More and more men driving away from the plant. He walked back into the building and called the union office. The woman was sorry, but Mr. Martin was in conference.

He told himself that the smart thing to do was go home—well, not home, but to Lindy's. But he'd set his goal for ending it. He was thinking about fast jets heading east, a comfortable old boat, a flaxen-haired girl who was eager to go with him.

He found Bob Warren in his cubicle eating lunch. Mark Lingate sat with his feet on his desk, eating his sandwiches.

"What's the wobble?" he asked.

"Same old garbage," Warren said. "I dunno the exact reason."

"Think it'll be over soon?" he asked. Warren shrugged.

"I'm thinking about taking the rest of the day off," Tusk said.

"Oh, to be a union member," Lingate sighed. He wiped his hands on his handkerchief, dropped his feet to the floor. "I thought you were going over Seattle way."

"I decided not to," Tusk said.

"All right, electricians," the PA system bellowed, "let's get back to work." And immediately afterward the same message was delivered to the pipe fitters.

Lingate sighed and stood up. The swinging door banged and rattled behind him. Tusk waited for a few seconds. "We'll be leaving here in a day or so," he told Bob. "If I don't get a chance to tell

Leigh goodbye, give her my thanks for the good meals and the parties.''

"We? Lindy's going with you?"

"Yes."

"Good for you two," Bob said. "Hey, you'll keep in touch?"

"Sure."

"Try to drop by before you leave, huh?"

"We'll try. I'm sure Lindy would want to see you."

"Well," Bob said. "Up and at 'em."

"Mind if I use the telephone?"

"It's yours." Warren pushed the gate and it slammed into Mark Lingate, coming in.

"Sorry 'bout that," Bob said.

"No damage," Lingate said. "I forgot something." He rummaged in a desk drawer, got out some papers, went out again. Tusk used the telephone; Mr. Martin was still in conference.

By midafternoon he had decided that it was the longest day of his life. Repeated efforts to contact Martin by telephone had failed. He decided to make one more try. There was always another day, one not complicated by Martin's having to deal with a wobble. This time he was put through.

"Martin." He raised his voice, spoke in a forced whispery falsetto. "I want to talk with you."

"Speak up," Martin said. "Who is this?"

"I need to talk with you now," he said in the

high sibilant voice. "It is very important to me, but it is more important to you. I want you to meet me—"

"Either tell me who this is or freak off," Martin said.

"Martin, listen." He started with the highest figure. "Two hundred thousand dollars. The Nucleospace Corporation." He named two more in descending order. "Do I have your attention?"

After a long pause Martin said grudgingly, "Yes."

"I will meet you in fifteen minutes."

"Listen, I have people here. We've had a wobble. I can't come now, damn it."

"I'm very patient."

"Later. Give me a number. I'll call you."

He chuckled in that forced high way. "Name a time, Martin. I'll call you."

"I don't know. It could take hours."

"Name a time, Martin, and be sure you can keep it."

"All right. Eight o'clock. Not here in the plant."

"Oh, yes, here in the plant. I'll call you." He hung up. Jesus. Eight o'clock. Five hours. He left the plant, stopped in the joint that was a favorite of the plant workers. A few of the electricians and pipe fitters who had taken advantage of the wobble for a day off were playing pinball for beers. He called Lindy from a booth, told her that he'd be a little late.

"Is everything all right?" she asked, concern in her voice.

"Yes. Don't worry."

"What time can I expect you?"

"I can't say. Just wait for me."

He had a beer, only one, made it last, spent some time driving, ended up on a hill overlooking the flatness of the site. It all looked small from up there, the two big private-company projects, one showing the bare bones of girders and framework, the other looking as if it were finished, but a chaos of incompletion inside. Far away the government reactors looked tiny along the river. The fast-flux plant was letting steam, or smoke, from a stack.

But his musing thoughts could not stay long from Lindy. Was she packing? Did she have a little smile on her face as she thought of leaving this place, leaving behind all the stresses and the tragic memories?

He lay down on the bunk in back and dozed, wristwatch alarm set as a precaution—a needless one, for the change in the light woke him to look out over evening, to see the sun disappear behind the western ridges.

There was risk. Because of his association with Lindy, having met her often at the guard gate, some of the guards knew him, knew that he had spent a lot of time with Frank Pitt's widow. But if it looked too risky there was always the cavalry. He could call for help, and it wouldn't hurt his pride, not now, not when it was ending and it was the last. But it was an unfamiliar face at the gate when he showed his badge and went in, making his way to the big building.

There were fewer people in the plant at night. Lights illuminated most areas with a white glare. The pace, slow enough by day, seemed even slower as night-shift workers carried on toward the long-delayed completion of the unit. He waited until exactly eight. It was Martin who answered the telephone.

"Up top," he said, in the forced high voice.

"All right," Martin said. No strain in his voice.

He had made the call from a telephone near the top, and now took the stairs up, hid in shadows and waited. Martin came in the elevator. He looked just slightly rumpled, as if it had been a bad day. He walked into the open space and looked around. The elevator stayed at the top. If it started back down Tusk could hear it. He had positioned himself to be able to see the stairwell. He didn't really expect Martin to bring company, not on the first encounter. He'd be too worried, too curious to know how big the bite was going to be.

He gave it five minutes, and Martin was still alone. He lit a cigarette and the flare of the lighter in the shadows caused Martin to start slightly. Then he walked out.

Martin didn't speak until they were face to face, a yard apart. There was no indication of nervousness in his voice. He came out punching. "One telephone call and you're dead," he said.

"But you haven't made that call," Tusk said. "You won't make it, because I'm not greedy."

"I'll have to know how you found out," Martin said.

"You're not in a position to make demands." Tusk blew smoke toward Martin's face.

"What's your proposition?" Martin asked. "How much?"

"Why, Mr. Martin," Tusk said with a grin, "do I look like a blackmailer?"

The first indication of doubt crossed Martin's face. "I'm not in the mood for games."

"Neither am I. All I want from you is the reason why you killed or had killed a man named Frank Pitt."

Martin knitted his brows. "You're crazy."

"He was after you," Tusk said. "He knew you were putting the arm on the company. What did he tell you? To knock it off and get out of the plant before he blew the whistle?"

"Look, if you're police, this is stupid. I had nothing to do with that. Hell, I can prove that I wasn't even in the plant when he fell."

"As you said, one telephone call."

"Listen, damn it, I tell you I had nothing to do with it. I had no reason for wanting Pitt dead. If this is what you've called me up here to talk about, you're wasting your time. You said some things that got my attention, but nothing to do with murder. Now if you want to talk business and if you're not greedy—''

Tusk didn't allow him to finish. He moved quickly, caught Martin by surprise, had his arm twisted up behind his back with enough pressure to cause the smaller man to grunt in pain and rise onto his toes.

"Martin, it happened right here. Right up here." He pushed. Martin resisted, but was moved forward, feet scuffling. Tusk pushed Martin's belt hard against the guardrail at the edge of the equipment bay. "Right here in this spot," he said. "He went over right here and he fell down, and down, and he hit down there. Do you see the spot?''

"You crazy son of a—"

"Tell me why and how, Martin," Tusk said. "And please talk fast, because I'd hate to push you over without hearing it from you."

"Listen, let's talk, huh? We can work something out. I tell you that I didn't do it and I didn't have it done."

Tusk put pressure on the arm.

"Now, damn it, that hurts," Martin said, total surprise in his voice. He wasn't used to being hurt.

"Talk," Tusk said.

"I'm talking, I'm talking. I had nothing to do with it. Far as I know he fell—"

Martin's voice failed him, because in one quick movement Tusk had lifted him, one hand holding him by the seat of his tailored pants, the other at the neck, shirt and coat clasped in his hand. He lifted, balanced Martin as he struggled, bumped his stomach on the guardrail. The man was cool. After the initial struggle he was quite still.

"If someone did push him," Martin said in a quiet calm voice, "you're going to kill the wrong man."

"Martin, Martin," he said in a coaxing voice. "It's over." Okay, give the man a little bit of incentive to talk, a little bit of hope. "Tell me why and how. Then we'll take the elevator down and we'll call the police and it'll be your word against mine. You'll have a chance that way. This way your only chance is that maybe you'll faint as you fall and won't feel it when you hit."

"Listen, please listen to me. If you force me to say I killed him, I will. But for the last time, damn it, I didn't. I had no reason. You're the first one who's come to me. My differences with Pitt were just union involvements."

He had a sick feeling. It had a ring of truth.

"Look, I have contacts, Smith. With the police and elsewhere. If it isn't money you want I'll help you find out who did it. We'll turn this place upside down."

He sighed. He was as sure as sure that once again he'd been wrong. Martin's tacit admission of guilt in demanding kickbacks from contractors was not important. What was important was that he was back at the beginning, and maybe, just maybe, there was no killer. Maybe Frank had just been brave, tried to look over the edge to try to prove that he wasn't afraid or something. Maybe—

There was a burst of sound in his head. It was a meaty, solid sound of impact, the kind of sound Frank's body may have made on the cement. He tried to lunge backward, to drag Martin with him, felt the strength go out of his hands, heard that sound again and was sinking down into whiteness that turned black. He felt, just before he felt nothing, his fingers go limp, knew in that split second before he crumpled down inside the guardrail that Martin was falling, but he heard no scream, heard nothing.

There was no way to know how long before one eyelid twitched, and through the greatest effort of his life he was able to roll his eyes downward from where they seemed to be implanted in his skull, to see a dimness, an unfocused view of a foot. Not his. It moved. His foot was incapable of movement, his entire body limp, signals going out from his brain to be ignored by his hands, his legs. He felt something, felt a shifting of his body, and the motion sent a surge of bile into his throat, and he couldn't swallow, felt that shifting, felt himself seeming to float, and she was there and saying words that didn't register, but it was her voice, and there was fear and shock in it, and there was a tape recorder in his numbed brain taking it all down. He felt a thud as he was dropped to the floor, and now there was another set of feet, and Lindy was crying out, and another voice that he couldn't quite hear. He saw her then, falling into the limited vision of his one open eye, long flaxen hair in motion, head striking the cement to lie still, the hair falling still to become motionless, and then that floating feeling again and a hardness in his gut as he was bent, brain fighting desperately to think, realizing at last that he lay over the guardrail, head and arms hanging limply to point toward the floor five hundred feet below.

He seemed to be suspended there for an eternity, and then there was motion again and he was sliding, sliding, brain dulled, not even frantic, just knowing, feeling the beginning of motion and a cool passage of air and the knowledge that he was falling, his old training there in that dulled brain beginning the count drilled into him, hup tousand, tup— Impossible. For a moment the great jarring impact sent tendrils of terror into his mind, and then he was in total blackness that faded with the twitching of his left eyelid.

He was lying on hardness, not smooth, his legs jammed, chest hurting, breathing causing a fiery pain that began to seep through the misty blackness. He did not try to move. Something in him told him not to move. He let only his eyes move, forcing them down, down, trying to lift the one-ton weight of eyelids. After a few years of it he could see. He could see a long, long distance to the floor below, and there were men cluttered around something that glistened red. He moved a hand experimentally, found a piece of metal, gripped it hard willing himself back to consciousness.

He had struck the boom of a crane left extended out into the equipment bay. He didn't know how far he'd fallen. But his head was toward the base of the crane, and when he had the strength he'd be able to crawl down the boom to safety. Meanwhile something nagged at him, a swift jab of pure fear. He closed his eyes and tried to make his breathing shallow to lessen the pain in his chest.

"Oh, no, God, no."

It played back, far back in his brain, her voice filled with fear and despair. He could not have stopped it if he'd wanted to; he listened to his memories with growing pain. He heard, in that dark part of his brain that, in an eerie, delayed, inexplicable way, was remembering what it had registered. He heard another voice, the one he could not recognize.

"—sorry you came here."

"You tried to kill—"

"—shouldn't have—Lindy."

"Don't make it worse—don't—"

"—late—loved you, worshipped you—teased me—gave yourself to this—"

He was reaching out, finding handholds as he lay at a downward angle. His legs were heavy. He inched himself down the boom and the thing kept playing in his brain.

"—talk—over here and we'll talk—"

"—late—saw—loved you so much—said you were lonely—how many—screwed because—lonely—"

"—come away—talk—all right—" Her voice pleading. She falling into limited vision, head on the cement. And he was crawling with his hands on rough metal edges as he regained more and more control, reaching the base of the crane, solidity underfoot, then the cement floor that rippled only slightly, his chest hurting. At least two broken ribs, and his vision coming and going.

The elevator took forever to reach him, and it was empty and no one noticed him as he staggered out one level from the ground. Men were crowding into the elevator in delayed reaction as he reached ground level, down the stairs, other men out there around that redness. The fresh air of the night helped his dizziness, but not the pain in his chest. He reached the guard's post after only a hundred miles of walking.

"Did you see Mrs. Pitt?"

"Yes, sure did. Went out with a fellow from start-up. She looked pretty sick. He was holding her up. Said she had passed out and he was taking her home."

"In what?" he asked.

"Four-wheeler. Scout."

Lindy's Scout. She liked driving it, used it more

often than she used the sedan. He went out the gate. His van was all the way on the other side of the compound, in the other lot. But there was a guard vehicle parked in front of the guard post. Maybe the same Toyota jeep in which he'd ridden with Lindy so long ago. He glanced in and saw the key in the ignition, heard the shout from behind him as he scratched gravel and shot out of the parking lot.

The access road leading to the highway was empty in front of him. And she'd seen the killer cause Martin's death, had seen him trying to lift Tusk's own body to toss him over. "I'm sorry you came." That's what the killer had told her. "It's too late. You saw."

But where would he take her to kill her, too? Unless he had happened to look up, he would have thought that his two victims were both dead. Now he would cover his tracks—reluctantly, because he'd said he loved her.

Out there on the highway there was traffic. And here, just ahead, a dirt road turned to angle off into the reservation. He could hear activity behind him as he braked, stood up and looked out over the moonlit flatness of the desert. There, about two miles off, topping a rise. No lights, but a dark shape outlined briefly atop the rise, heading down toward the river, a big river, a river that could accept a woman's small body easily.

He doused his own lights, took the dirt road slowly at first, then increasingly fast as his eyes became more adjusted to the moonlight. His chest was hurting and he could feel a stickiness at the back of his neck running down inside his shirt. He remembered the road from his sightseeing tour with the lady guard, the lady who loved him, who had become concerned about him and had come to seek him at the plant. How had she known to come to the top? Had she guessed that that was where it would happen? That he'd lure Frank's killer there? However it had happened, she had come and now she was out there somewhere.

He could not see the Scout from the top of the rise on which he'd spotted it, dashed on, heading toward the river, taking the loop down there to see nothing, watching closely, a part of his mind praying that the killer would want to talk, to tell her how sorry he was that he was going to have to kill her. She'd been quite cool after the initial shock up there at the five-hundred-foot level; maybe she could delay it, keep him talking. Behind him there were car lights.

He did not see the Scout along the river. The moon was huge, full, incredibly bright, making the desert seem to gleam in its light, making very good visibility. He glanced behind as he turned away from the river, saw the lights of two vehicles. He passed one of the old radioactive dumps, a high mound, sand and tumbleweed and sagebrush growing atop buried poison. He guessed, then, what was in the killer's mind.

He pressed down on the accelerator and bounced over a rough rise and saw the Scout up ahead, parked near one of the large mounds. They'd hear him coming. He was in time. He could hope now, for she'd be with him soon, and it would be over, and Frank's murderer had shown his hand, and even if he had to let the courts decide punishment it was over and all he had to do was get there before—

The steering wheel wrenched hard at his hands and arms as a front wheel hit a hole, a rock, soft sand, something, and the pain in his chest was a lance that made the moonlight flame, and the jeep was slewing and he felt himself going, going, the vehicle flipping over as he was thrown clear to land with a roaring, burning and all-consuming pain that he felt for only a moment. And now he'd spent two lifetimes trying to open his left eye. But all was softness and old familiar faces and quiet voices that tried to burn through and didn't. He could hear a voice talking to him— "G.W., G.W." He tried to answer and heard the croak of his own voice, and it seemed to help, hearing it, for he could see, and it was Mandy Pitt with one of his hands in her dry old hands, bending down.

"You hear me now, don't you, G.W.?"

"Yes."

"I told them you were tough."

"Lindy—"

"Hush, hush." Another face, strange but feminine and kind, and a sip of the best water of his life through a straw, and the dampness in his throat and pain there, too, but he didn't know about the tubes until later.

Mandy was still there. "Lindy . . ." he began.

"Hush. You've been hurt very badly. You need all your strength. It's all right. Everything's all right."

He felt quite small, and her voice seemed to come from far away, but later it was closer and he was larger and he could use both eyes. Nurses gave him only a sip of water, just enough to tease him, to dampen his parched lips. Doctors needled him, fed him through a tube, kept him on the edge of awareness.

At last he was awake enough, allowed to be alert enough to insist; and it was Mandy, eyes wet, her dry, soothing old hands holding one of his, who told him.

PITT, BELINDA (MRS. FRANK), nee BELINDA ALICE ECKHART, former MRS. ARNOLD DORR, never to be MRS. G.W. SMITH, was dead.

He left the hospital in two weeks, leaning on the arms of two old ladies, Mandy Pitt's head coming not even to his shoulder, Anna Larch, the stronger, supporting most of his weight. The world was altogether too bright, too harsh. He seemed to be looking at it through the small end of a telescope. He was a thousand feet tall, and he tottered, had to use his hands to lift his heavy legs and feet into the van. He was pleased to see the bed in the room at Anna's, slept quickly.

He wanted to know. Bob Warren came. The police and state people had stopped coming after the first few days in the hospital when he could talk. He wanted to know everything, and Bob Warren talked with the supervisor, Abe Johnson, and Johnson came with all the details and even pictures and was gruff to cover his discomfort. So he knew.

It was a hundred miles to the backyard, then the distance came down to fifty and then ten, and his feet weighed only a hundred pounds each. Anna and Mandy were trying to fatten him, put back on the lost weight, but his slacks were still too loose when he looked up from the lounge chair under the shade of a tree in the backyard and saw a tanned woman with tawny, sun-streaked hair. She wore a sundress that showed her shoulders, sandals, no hose.

"This lady says she's from the company that employs you," Mandy said.

"Yes, hi," he said.

"Don't you think you've given these two nice ladies enough trouble?" Zed asked.

"Yes." For a moment it crossed his mind that they'd sent Zed because he'd told them he was getting out. He tried to laugh at himself. They didn't work that way.

"You're going to stay right where you are, G.W. Smith," Mandy said. "We're perfectly capable of taking care of you."

"You're wonderful," he said to her. "You're my one true love, Mandy."

"Fickle," Anna said. "You told me that only yesterday."

He uncoiled from the lounge chair, his head not nearly as far from the ground as it had been for so long. "Mandy, you need to get back to your diving."

"I'll see to it that he gets the best of care," Zed told them, all sweetness, all brown from the sun, a smile on her face that he knew from experience she used only as a con. Zed was not a smiler.

"Well, if you're sure, G.W.," Mandy said.

He didn't know why he was going with her, almost wished that his whimsical thought was based on truth, would have welcomed it. She didn't speak until, she driving his van, they were headed north.

"I think you'd do the same for me," she said.

"I don't know."

"They send their best wishes, the four. The case is closed."

"When did you get here?" he asked.

"In time to spend most of the night waiting in the hospital to see if you were going to survive surgery."

"They sent you out anyhow, huh?"

"You'd lost your objectivity." She looked at him coldly. "I think you were in love."

"Think what you please," he said, and there was no more talk.

The cottage was tucked away on the brink of a deep canyon. Behind it the desert stretched for miles to a distant slope on which there was irrigated green. In front was the gorge and far below a ribbon of water in the stream. It was cool and quiet, and she left him alone. His walks were limited to the small rocky yard for a while, then he began to branch out. She seemed happy to be alone, spent her time lying in the sun, baking herself to a degree that would have made huge blisters on his own skin. He read in the evening or watched whatever he wanted to see on the TV set. They spoke only when necessary. She was a surprisingly good cook and ate with a hearty appetite.

"Look, you don't have to stay here," he told her at the end of a week, when he was walking a half mile at a time and beginning to help with the cooking and the cleaning up afterward.

"Okay," she said. She came out of her bedroom in ten minutes with a packed bag. She put the bag down, turned to the chair in which he was sitting. "Are you still going to quit?"

He didn't answer for a moment. It didn't really matter. He shrugged.

She laughed. "And they keep saying you're the best."

He did not speak.

"The best." She made a snorting sound. "You blew it in North Carolina two years ago, and if it hadn't been for me you'd have lost a client. You blew it in Arizona. I had to come to the rescue. You blew it here and lost your girl."

It was true. His anger was unreasonable. He rose too quickly, felt a sudden dizziness, took two steps toward her.

"You killed her because you'd gone soft," she said.

If he could only reach her, get his hands on her, close them around her neck, make her eat those words. She danced away from him and he came to a halt, panting with effort.

"Look at you," she said, that cold beautiful face sneering at him. "The best. And you let a punk kill your girl. Sweet Lindy. Your love, Lindy."

"Shut up," he said.

"Went after the wrong man again, let the punk sneak up behind you and coldcock you, let him carry off your love."

"I will kill you," he said softly, with a conviction that seemed to have only the effect of putting that smile on her face, the con smile, the meaningless smile.

"Not even when you're healthy," she said. "Not even then. You can't even compete with a punk. And you let her play you for a sucker, as well, because she was screwing the punk."

He knew that he couldn't catch her, and if he did she was right. He couldn't take her in his condition.

"Please stay," he said.

"Oh?"

"I'm begging you to stay. Stay until I'm just half a man."

She laughed again, a harsh forced sound. "I don't have that much time. You're the best, letting a little housing-development buzz saw turn you into jelly, letting a little punk almost kill you and kill your sweet little buzz saw."

"Will you stay?"

"Are you sure that's the way you want it?" The look was one he'd seen before. What followed it had not been pleasant. He nodded. He needed something to hit, something to hate, because it was inside him, all the hate, and it was directed toward himself because he'd been wrong again. He'd gone after the wrong man, and that man had died; a man whose crime—greed, forcing money from the contractors—was not excusable, but did not call for a sudden stop after a fall of five hundred feet. He needed someone to hit because he had insisted on knowing, on seeing.

"In a couple of hundred years," Bob Warren had told him, speaking softly, reluctantly, "they may think about getting the bodies out."

At first he hadn't even known who it was, waking there in the hospital to see Mandy's ancient wrinkles. A state investigating agent had told him. And then it had all been clear, because Anna Larch had brought the last packet, the one he should have waited for before he started his final actions.

A woman stood there laughing at him in the huge, deeply carpeted living room of a desert cottage—if a couple of hundred thousand dollars' worth of luxury can be called a cottage—and he could see, superimposed over her face, the face of Lindy, the way he'd always see her face.

"We assume," the state agent had said, "that Lingate intended to kill Mrs. Pitt by forcing her to go into the bunker. She was in uniform when she came to the plant, most probably, according to your story, so that she would have free access to look for you. She had her keys, one of which, of course, fit the standard locks on the bunkers."

"If that's the way you want it," Zed said, smiling that con woman's smile, "I'll stay. I'll even help you get into condition. We'll see if you can direct some of that fine anger into getting yourself into shape instead of lying around mooning over a dead broad."

"You're very kind," he said.

"Starting now," she said.

She walked ahead of him, shoulders bared to the sun, and she walked swiftly. He followed doggedly, forcing himself, staying on his feet when he thought it was no longer possible. It was the beginning of a short stretch in hell. The endless walking, the taunting smile, food served to him with that smile, rubber balls thrust into his hands in the evenings when he was too exhausted to move, an order, a sneer, "Squeeze, damn you, squeeze."

When she began to run he lived through it only by picturing Lindy's face in his mind.

"I guess he was trying to push her into the radiation area," Bob Warren had said when Tusk insisted on knowing all. "You go around the right-angle radiation traps." Yes, he remembered Lindy herself telling him about it. The bunker into which, from a safe distance, they'd pulled the flatcars with old used-up but still highly radioactive reactor-core parts atop. Radiation in the hundreds of rems. You began to get blood changes at twenty-five rems. You take one step, then two, and you're dead and—

"What's the matter, Smith?" Zed was saying. She was in jogging shorts, legs long, deep brown. She was leaning over him as he lay gasping on the sand. "Think of your sweetie. One of the nuclear people told me that they won't even decay in there, that the radiation is so intense that it will kill all the bacteria. She'll be as good as new two hundred years from now, Smith, maybe just dried up a little."

On his feet, seeing it, seeing her face begin to dry, to wrinkle, a twentieth-century mummy with flaxen hair, following the pumping legs of brown with hate in his heart.

"Rock climbing today," Zed said, one early morning with the dew still on the brown sage. He made it down, swam in the stream below, made it to the top. He was tired, but he'd made it and his legs didn't tremble.

There came a day when he ran at her side, and she could not leave him behind. Stretched out, into that reserve of energy that comes only to those who can stand the pain of an oxygen-starved body, he almost as brown as she now, bare to the waist, legs flashing, artificial feet slinging slightly outward in an awkward gait that kept him up with her, staying with her until she stopped and fell off into a walk, her chest heaving.

Weights in the game room, pumping iron, she on the bench beside him using the same size weight for a while, until, things beginning to hum inside him, he advanced the weights.

Now there was a nip in the air. Snow had begun in the mountains, the higher passes closed, but there on the high desert it was only a coolness and there were times, when they ran, that he could forget for a moment and just feel his body, humming, long muscles stretched and powerful. But in the night he'd see it.

"They built an inspection port into the things," Bob Warren had said. "A sort of periscope affair with right angles and all, so's the radiation won't come out. You can see them. They're just inside and about four feet away from the entrance to the first trap."

"I want to go out there," he'd said.

"No, you don't, G.W. You don't want to do that."

"Yes."

"I don't think they'll let you," Bob had said.

"I have to see. I have to know."

"Boy, you're just punishing yourself. No one could have guessed that Mark was a fruitcake."

LINGATE, MARCUS W: Follow up report. ALERT.

Damn, if only he'd waited. It was spelled out there. There was—he'd never taken the trouble to find out who—a man who once theorized that the world existed only in his own mind; that if he perished, the entire world, the universe, perished with him. And there were those who talked about that mishmash as a serious philosophical concept. And there were those among us who, without knowing they were feeling it, lived that concept, a twist somewhere in the mind making them the center of the universe, leaving all others outside to be mere objects to be manipulated. Some devoted the talent to making money and amassed vast fortunes. Others achieved success in the arts. Still others carried it a bit further and tried to fulfill their personal needs in other manners. The death of a man had no reality to such a person. If death suited the purpose of such a person, and if accomplishing that purpose carried no danger of reprisal by a society that he held in contempt, then it was death.

Marcus Lingate had left a trail behind him, a trail that was evident in the secondary material marked, by Oscar, ALERT. Each incident, examined separately, could have been dismissed as

coincidence. An overall view by one who had encountered such things before showed an unmis-
takable pattern. A childhood friend, rival for the
last spot open on a Little League baseball team,
drowned, and he had been an excellent swim-
mer. Lingate had been twelve at the time, and
old newspaper clippings quoted him as being
heartbroken, quoted him as saying that he'd
tried to save his friend. But then he lost a girl in
high school, a girl who had been going steady
with him. The car went over an oceanside cliff,
but Lingate was thrown clear into brush atop the
drop. And at his college the man who was neck
and neck with him and a bit ahead for the top
graduation honors unexpectedly committed suicide by blowing his brains out with a Saturday-
night special.

One had to speculate about the girl, but Mark
had wanted the spot on the baseball team, and
he'd got it. He'd wanted the college honors, and
won them by default. He'd wanted Lindy.

"We found written matter and snapshots, Pola-
roid pictures, in Lingate's room, pretty good indication that he'd been having an affair with Mrs.
Pitt," the state investigator had said. "Poems,
yet. Poems you wouldn't believe. Poems promis-
ing her that she would be with him always, and
soon. No way to prove it, but I'd bet my hat and
ass he pushed Frank Pitt. He wanted Pitt out of
the way because, judging from some of those pictures, which were pretty hot, Mrs. Pitt gave him

good reason. Then she took up with you, and he came after you."

He did not want to see those pictures, but he saw them. Lindy, the model, but not high fashion; the pictures, in the crude medium, taken by an amateur, having the vulgar touch of lust and nakedness. He would never know if the affair had ended before he met her or if it had continued afterward and if, for example, Lindy had been the one to drop the hint, perhaps unintentionally, that G.W. Smith suspected murder in Frank's death. And how had Lingate known that he and Lindy were planning to go away? There was that day when he told Bob Warren, and Lingate came back into the cubicle just as Bob was leaving. Had he been standing outside the door? There were other pictures.

"Listen, Tusk, I think I know how you feel," Warren had said. "I guess if it were me I'd want to see her, too. Maybe I can borrow the pictures."

"I've seen some pictures." Legs open, a leering smile on her face.

"These were taken through the inspection device. You can see Lindy's face. She's in her uniform."

"We can only theorize," the state investigator had said, "that he was trying to kill her by pushing her into the radioactive bunker, past the radiation traps. Apparently she fought and grabbed him, and he lost his balance and they both went stumbling in together."

There by the swimming pool, an aeon or so ago, he had pretended that he was going to push her in, and her reaction was swift, clinging to him instinctively. Then she'd pulled them both in, laughing.

She wasn't laughing in the pictures that they showed him. She had fallen onto her back, one leg thrown out to the side. Lingate was atop her, his body between her legs. Her face showed clearly, her eyes open, startled, her lips parted in what had the look of a kiss. And in a couple of hundred years they might think about taking her desiccated body out of that embrace of death, Lingate's body atop her drying out, not even any bacteria to cause them to decay, deprived, for a long, long time, of the right to follow the biblical injunction of dust to dust.

"Not bad for a cripple," Zed said as they returned from an evening run, a cold wind coming down from the plains and mountains to the north.

He didn't hate her. He had used up all the hate he had. He'd poured it into the agonizing weeks in which she'd forced him, by taunting him, to punish his body up and away from the punctured lung and broken ribs and internal injuries that had almost killed him. She came out of the shower in a towel. She'd never been one to show modesty, although there was nothing sensual in it. He knew her as a killing machine, a cold woman. He had finished first and was dressed in slacks and shirt. He handed her a tall gin and tonic. She looked at him with one raised eyebrow.

"There's hope for you yet," she said. "I could teach you manners if I had time."

He grinned. "Thank you," he said.

"Don't go emotional on me." She stared at him coldly.

"Did you decide to take me to raise on your own, or did they—"

"They know where I am," she said quickly.

"Thank you again. Now you can go. Really."

"Well, was it all a waste?" she asked. "Are you still going to quit?"

He'd been thinking about that. "Zed, I was wrong three times."

"You were in love the last time."

"Don't say anything else about her," he said.

"No. But we've all been wrong at times. You've just had a string of them."

"I'm not even sure they'll still want me," he said.

"They want you. You're the best."

He grinned again. "Ah, so you admit it?"

"To hell with you," she said, with the only genuine little smirk of a smile he'd ever seen on her. "What about it? Do we report in?"

"No," he said. "You report in. I'm going fishing."

A quick anger altered her face for only a moment. "I'm going to tell you something very few people know," she said.

"You don't have to."

"I think I do, because there aren't many like us. Because I can't forget, as you seem to be able to do." She held up her hand as he started to protest. "It happened when I was twenty-two. The all-girl jock, tennis, track, golf. He was a high-school football coach, my husband, a little older. We had a typical development house and two atypical little girls in that they were mine and therefore something special, and we were making house payments and car payments and were so damned happy we didn't care, and then they came in one night while we were sleeping, three of them. They killed my two atypical little girls first, then they killed my husband, and then they took me. They kept me for three days. Three of them. One day when we were moving in a car I hit the one beside me in the throat with the back of my hand, which I'd been hardening at night by beating on my bed, holding the handcuffs with the other hand so they wouldn't jingle. I went out the door and hit the road and went over a drop, and they didn't come down to look for me because I was supposed to be dead after falling a couple of hundred feet, but I wasn't. I was just scratched up. The organization found me after I'd tracked down the last two."

"What do I say, Zed?"

"There are still people like those animals out there," she said. "You think you hurt. Well, after twelve years I still hurt. I try to think of things I should have done to prevent it. Locks, better locks on the doors of our happy little home." She turned away.

"I guess I need some time to think," he said. Jesus, Zed crying? He went to her, put his hands on her shoulders. She flinched, tried to move out from under. He turned her.

There were those, like the coordinator, who sometimes speculated about holding the tawny-haired woman close. There was a fascination in it, like cuddling up with a rattlesnake. But to Tusk she was just a woman, and there were tears on her cheeks, something he had thought he'd never see. He held her close and patted her on the back.

They flew east. October had come, and there were golden days as he steered the old boat southward along the intracoastal waterway. She spent a lot of time in the sun. They had reported in, and there were no assignments. They didn't talk much, drank little, did daily battle in calisthenics on the deck and hard, exhausting swimming in the water. And she baked herself, punished herself as the sun grew warmer in the South.

"Isn't it time you let up on yourself a little?" he asked one night, with the boat anchored in a bay. "You can't cook it away in the sun."

"I don't need advice," she said.

She was the most infuriating woman. He stepped close to her. "I think I know what you mean," he said. He had his lips on her, quickly, before she exploded, her blows meant to be lethal, a cornered tigress; and before he subdued her with superior strength and weight he ached in a dozen places and wondered at the violence in her. She could have killed him with a blow to his larynx, could have ruined him for life with a knee to the groin.

"I'm going to turn you loose," he panted. "If you stop trying to kill me."

Her lips were pulled back, showing teeth clamped closely together. Slowly the hate faded from her eyes.

"I won't try that again," he said.

She lay on the bunk where they had fallen, her chest heaving. He mixed drinks. She sat up.

"Put the drinks down," she said, her voice cold.

"Peace," he said. He still ached. He'd have some bruises.

"Come here. Sit down."

"Yes, ma'am," he said meekly.

She put both hands on his face, turning his head toward her. Her kiss was tentative at first, then wet. She removed her hands. "Yes," she said. He raised his eyebrows. "You started it," she said. "Now finish it. It's been twelve years."

It was almost as violent as the brief but potentially deadly battle of minutes before, a form of combat without slashing hands and punching fingers and knees, and after she had cried out she pushed him away. She spent the next morning in the sun, top removed from her suit, not speaking, taking the tall glass of tea that he delivered at midmorning without looking up. In the afternoon he anchored and went into the water. They were secluded. He didn't wear a swimsuit, just the fins, and she joined him, standing for a moment outlined against the sky, a tall brown-skinned woman with a tiny splash of white at breasts and groin, and then she was cutting the water out and away, far away, so that he was concerned until she started back and came panting, the last of her strength going as he helped her up to the deck.

She spoke as they ate freshly caught fish at twilight, the meat cooked on a charcoal fire topside. "It wasn't you," she said. "I couldn't see your face or feel your body. It was—"

"I know. Your husband."

She came to his bunk, skin cool, bare. But after the initial combat there was a warm sweetness, a giving, a shared night that left them at peace, to be awakened by the heat building up in the cabin in the noontime sun.

She left him in Key West. One of the periodic checks with Oscar took her away. There was a particularly nasty one in southern Ohio, one that called for a woman's touch.

She stood on the deck dressed in a little beige suit, browned legs encased in hose for the first time in weeks.

"I'm not supposed to tell you," he said, "but I talked to Oscar, too. They've asked me to stand by in case you need help up there."

"Thanks," she said, turning to give him the non-con smile.

"If it turns out to be simple I'll be here around the Keys somewhere," he said.

"Thanks again," she said. She came to him, did not have to tiptoe to peck a little kiss on his lips. "But I think not, don't you?"

"I guess so."

"Your name isn't Jim and mine isn't Lindy," she said.

He watched her walk away, up the dock, get into a taxi. As a matter of fact, he didn't even know her name.

Move to

RAVEN HOUSE

**Home of the Finest
in Mystery Reading!**

The ALL NEW series of crime and suspense!

Millions of fans
can't be wrong...

For more than a century and a half,
tales of mystery and detection
have captured the imaginations
of readers the world over.

RAVEN HOUSE
MYSTERIES ...

...offers the finest examples
of this entertaining popular fiction—
in a brand-new series that contains
everything from puzzling whodunits
to stories of chilling suspense!

Reviewers across the country rave about Raven House!

"...impressive writing..."
—*Ellery Queen Magazine*

"...a joy to suspense buffs."
—*West Coast Review of Books*

"...fiendishly clever..."
—*Quality*

"...well worth the [price]..."
—*Jessyca Russell Gaver's Newsletter*

"...the best news in years for the paperback mystery field."
—*Wilson Library Bulletin*